CW01572605

"HESS? WHICH HESS?..."

Eric Sturdy

Mouse Gate Press

Mouse Gate Press
284 The Circle
Queen Elizabeth Street, London SE1 2JW
011 44 796 638 0131
www.MouseGate.com

All rights reserved. Except as permitted under the United States Copyright Act of 1976, No part of this publication may be reproduced, stored in a retrieval system, or transmitted in any form or by any means electronic or mechanical or by photocopying, recording, or otherwise without prior permission of the publisher. Exclusive worldwide content publication / distribution by TotalRecall Publications, Inc.

Copyright © 2014 by: Eric Sturdy
All rights reserved
ISBN   978-1-59095-092-0
UPC: 6-43977-20925-2

Library of Congress # 9781590950920
Printed in the United States of America with simultaneous printings in Australia, Canada, and United Kingdom.

FIRST EDITION
1   2   3   4   5   6   7   8   9   10

This is a work of fiction. The characters, names, events, views, and subject matter of this book are either the author's imagination or are used fictitiously. Any similarity or resemblance to any real people, real situations or actual events is purely coincidental and not intended to portray any person, place, or event in a false, disparaging or negative light.

The scanning, uploading and distribution of this book via the Internet or via any other means without the permission of the publisher is illegal and punishable by law. Please purchase only authorized electronic editions, and do not participate in or encourage electronic piracy of copyrighted materials. Your support of the author's rights is appreciated.

This historical fictional novel is dedicated to my younger grandchildren –

James, Harry and Megan Sturdy
William and Brodie Coghlan
and my one and only great grandchild, Frankie.

Acknowledgements

Published works were perused on the mysteries surrounding Rudolf Hess and tribute is paid to the following – William L. Shire's illustrated history, "The Rise and Fall of the Third Reich" (1987); Dr Hugh Thomas's two publications, "The Murder of Rudolf Hess" (1979) and "A Tale of Two Murders" (1988); Gita Severing's mammoth tome, "Albert Speer – His Battle with the Truth" (1995), and Stephen McGinty's recent publication, "Camp Z: The Secret Life of Rudolf Hess" (2011). A list of acknowledgements would not be complete without reference to my researchers, proofreaders and typist who were immensely helpful in preparing this work for publication. Dr Alun Rolfe, a retired psychiatrist at Maindiff Court, facilitated a visit to inspect Hess's quarters at the hospital and introduced me to Joseph Clifford, a Pioneer guard at Maindiff during the war. Sadly, Joe Clifford passed away in 2011, and his recollection of his wartime experiences were extremely helpful. Mr Forbes Rintoul, a surgical colleague, provided valuable information about Hess's time in captivity at Abergavenny. Mr Stephen Barber, a well-known local historian, undertook the galling task of detailed research and proofreading and provided the title for this work. Without the expertise of my granddaughters, Claire Whitefield and Sarah Turnham, my book would not have seen the light of day. Joint directors of "Wonder Company", a highly successful advertising agency in Newport, South Wales, they facilitated the production side of my venture. One of their staff, Miss Katie Lloyd, produced the cover. The typing was undertaken by Miss Hannah Webb, and I am indebted for her expertise. Finally, I extend my grateful thanks to Chris MacNeil for supervising publication of my work.

Introduction

AT THE PALACE OF JUSTICE IN NUREMBERG IN OCTOBER 1945 THERE WERE TWENTY-THREE TOP NAZI WARTIME LEADERS ON TRIAL FOR WAR CRIMES. The Court was in session for eleven months and the indicted Nazis were seated in two rows. 'Rudolf Hess' sat in the front row flanked by Reichsmarschal Hermann Göering in pole position on his right hand and Joachim von Ribbentrop, Germany's Foreign Minister, on his left-hand side. It seemed pre-destined that the twelve prisoners in the front row would face execution at the end of the trial. As it transpired eleven were convicted to death by hanging and Rudolf Hess was awarded a life sentence. The true identity of the man seated in their midst in the dock at Nuremberg was repeatedly questioned by Göering and von Ribbentrop, each of whom had close connections with Hess before his defection to Britain in May 1941. Hermann

Göering was amused when an attorney spoke to him about Hess. Göering remarked, "Hess? Which Hess? The Hess you have here? Our Hess? Your Hess?" and Von Ribbentrop was recorded in conversation, "Hess? You mean Hess? The Hess we have here? But Hess did not know me! I look at him. I talk to him. Obviously he does not know me. It is just not possible. Nobody could fool me like that!"

During his National Service in Berlin the author served as Prison Medical Officer for three separate months in 1952 and 1953 when his Welsh Guards Battalion was on guard duty at Spandau. Prison visits were almost a daily occurrence and the author saw Prisoner No.7, allegedly Rudolf Hess, on a regular basis. At the time he had no inkling that No.7 was not Rudolf Hess. Over the years the author has come to a conclusion that No.7 at Spandau was a doppelgänger, an impostor in German, a view strongly supported by Hermann Göering's and von Ribbentrop's suspicions at Nuremberg. Why the judiciary and prison authorities did not take action at the Tribunal remains one of the enduring mysteries surrounding Rudolf Hess. Both Göering and von Ribbentrop met with the ultimate fate predicted for them before the Trial began. Göering cheated the gallows by taking a cyanide capsule in his cell a couple of hours before he was due to hang. Joachim von Ribbentrop and ten of his Nazi brethren were executed by hanging at the Palace of Justice at Nuremberg on the 14th October 1946. They were immediately cremated and their ashes were taken for dispersal at sea.

Apart from the mystery surrounding the identity of the Nazi prisoner at the Nuremberg Tribunal and Spandau Prison, various other unanswered, controversial enigmas about Germany's one-time Deputy Fuhrer remain. Access to the Nazi convicts for family visits was allowed at frequent intervals and less so at Spandau Prison. Rudolf Hess, or an impostor, steadfastly refused to meet with them until he was at death's door in December 1969. Treated at the British Military Hospital in Berlin he made a miraculous recovery and survived as the sole occupant of Spandau Prison for a further eighteen years. Hess's life was terminated on August 17th, 1987 when he was discovered hanging in a garden hut in the prison's exercise compound. Even this episode is shrouded in mystery and controversy exists as to whether "Hess" was murdered by a person, or persons, unknown or hung himself. If it transpires "Hess" was a doppelgänger, a major mystery remains as to why he refused to disclose his true identity and persisted with the charade in captivity for 41 years. The author's experience in providing medical supervision for the "Hess" at Spandau in 1952-53 created an abiding interest in his fate and has ultimately led to the production of this work.

THE SPANDAU SEVEN
MAY 1952 - JULY 1953

"Hessco" is the modern-day nickname for a Tesco supermarket built in 1988 on the site of Berlin's Spandau prison. the gaol was demolished in the autumn of 1987 on the death of its most famous, or according to divergent beliefs infamous, prisoner. Adolf Hitler's Deputy Führer, or an impostor, was sentenced to life imprisonment at the War Crimes Tribunal in Nuremberg and, of the seven senior Nazis given sentences, Prisoner No. 7 was the only one to see the end of his life in captivity. He was popularly thought to be Rudolf Hess but, over the years, suggestive evidence has accumulated to indicate otherwise and prisoner No. 7 may have conceivably been an impostor. Likewise there is considerable controversy about the manner of Prisoner No. 7's demise. Whether he hanged himself in a garden shed in Spandau or a person, or persons, hovering in the background aided the frail 92-year-old Nazi in his terminal passage to Valhalla, remains a mystery. The prison in Charlottenberg was demolished immediately after his death to avoid it becoming a place of worship for Nazi sympathisers. Rather than referring to the supermarket at Spandau as "Hessco" it might be more aptly renamed "Prostco" by using Prost, the surname of Hess's fictional impostor.

At the cessation of hostilities in Europe in May 1945 the four Allied Powers had agreed that Germany should be divided into two occupation zones roughly separated along the river Elbe, where the Allied armies came to rest. Much to Winston

Churchill's displeasure this meant that Berlin became an isolated enclave inside the Russian-dominated Eastern Zone, 45 kilometres inside the line of demarcation. The eastern half of the city came under Communist control and the western half of Berlin was divided into three sectors, each occupied by British, French and American forces. Access into Berlin from the west was restricted to one major highway, one rail link only used twice a week and flights along predestined air corridors to Gatow and Templehof airports. The British sector of the city was in the northwest Charlottenberg district and included the Brandenburg Gate, half of Kufurstendam Avenue, a British Military Hospital, S.S. army barracks and Spandau Prison. Built in the late 1860s the prison consisted of an outer high wall fortified by six guard turrets and separated from the main prison building by a dry moat festooned with barbed wire obstacles. The prison itself had three separate three-storied cellblocks all capable of housing 130 convicts and each with its own administrative offices. A sizeable exercise yard was situated at the rear of the cellblock and a section of the land had been cordoned-off to create a walled vegetable garden. In its heyday Spandau Prison could accommodate up to 600 inmates. Seven convicted Nazis were brought from Nuremberg to the prison in August 1947 and occupied separate cells on the first floor of the central prison block. The four Allied Powers took it in turns to mount guard on the prison for a month each quarter. The battalion designated for guard duty also supplied a medical officer to attend at the prison. The prisoners' daily schedule, diet, and health were monitored by prison warders and, on the last Friday every month, a Four-Power administrative and medical meeting was held to discuss the prisoners' complaints. The prison had a Commandant and in 1952, it had 22 permanent staff-warders, medical orderlies, cooks and cleaners. The average cost for running the specialised detention centre during this period was in the region of £85,000 a year.

The prisoners' monotonous daily routine was strictly regulated by rules drawn up by the War Crimes Commissioners at Nuremberg. Reveille was at 6.00am in the summer months and half an hour later in wintertime. After their ablutions, bed-making and tidying their cells, the prisoners went down to the dining room on the ground floor for breakfast at 8.00am, usually coffee, bread and cheese and occasionally a boiled egg. Weather permitting they then spent time during the morning out of doors in the exercise compound and vegetable garden. The main meal of the day was served at noon. After lunch the prisoners were locked in their cells for an hour's rest. Afternoons were again spent either in the exercise yard or reading and writing in a communal sitting room. At 5.00pm a light supper was served and afterwards the inmates were locked in their cells until lights out at 10.00pm. A visiting barber was on hand to shave the inmates twice a week. On Mondays they were expected to do their own laundry and on Sundays, a church service was conducted by a prison padre for the prisoners' benefit. Strictly enforced during the Russian duty months a diet of bread, soup, potatoes and coffee was adhered to day in and day out. The other three Powers varied the prisoners' diet and liberal protein and carbohydrate meals were on offer most days. Consumption of alcohol was strictly forbidden. The Nazi prisoners were allowed to write a censored one-page letter home per month and family visits were limited to 15 minutes every two months. A mini-library of historical, scientific and carefully selected literature and novels was available to prisoners in the Common Room. Within a few years some of these strict regulations had been relaxed by the Western Powers, mainly the edicts insisting on solitary confinement, dietary restrictions and two-hourly disturbance of their sleep at night. On their duty month Russian warders were prone to adhere strictly to the regulations laid down by the Nuremberg War Crimes Commissioners. Rudolf Hess had adhered fairly strictly to a vegetarian diet at Mytchett Place and Maindiff Court. His dietary requirements at the Palace of Justice in Nuremberg were well balanced and included a liberal supply of meat and fish products. It soon became evident at Spandau that 'Hess' had abandoned his vegetarian regime and was now an avid protein eater whenever it was available.

At the end of World War II in Europe, on 7th May 1945, the author was 17 years of age and eligible for conscription into the Armed Forces. At that time he was a second-year medical student at Guy's Hospital in London and the powers-that-be must have decided to let him qualify as a doctor and complete his internships before his call-up papers were issued – presumably because he would be of more value to His Majesty's forces as a doctor rather than a squaddie. His call to arms came in October of 1951. After 10 weeks basic training at the R.A.M.C Depot in Crookham, his posting to BAOR, the British Army on the Rhine, came through a week before Christmas 1951 and, on Christmas Eve, he joined as a Regimental Medical Officer, RMO, to the 1st Battalion Welsh Guards based at the time at Wuppertal. On March the 1st, 1952, his Guards' Battalion moved en bloc to the Charlottenberg district in West Berlin. Wavell Barracks was situated in close proximity to the British Military Hospital and Spandau Prison and, in April, the author was seconded to the surgical staff at the Hospital. The Welsh Guards were allocated guard duties at Spandau Prison during the months of May and September 1952 and January 1953 and, as their RMO, the author was automatically appointed Prison Medical Officer for these periods. His first attendance at Spandau Prison was on the 2nd of May 1952. He was instructed by the Hospital Commandant that the Nazi prisoners were only to be addressed by their cell numbers, one to seven, and not under any circumstances by their proper names. It was also stressed that the author was only to concern himself with medical complaints. The best suggested times for attendance on the prisoners would be late morning or at tea break after their compulsory rest period for an hour after lunch. Weather permitting, the prisoners were up-and-about in the exercise compound and in the vegetable garden or, otherwise, in the communal sitting room. If a prisoner was unwell he was allowed to remain in his cell or nursed in a twin-bedded Medical Inspection, MI, Room.

On the author's daily rounds to Spandau a Welsh Guards officer, usually a subaltern, and two guardsmen marched him down a short drive through the main prison gates and across a drawbridge over the moat to the prison entrance. A senior English-speaking warder then took over and led him to the Commandant's office to sign the attendance register. They then proceeded through two locked doors into the cellblock. The inmates were either in the exercise yard or in the Common Room with the exception of Prisoner No 7 who was rarely outside his cell. The author had to ask each in turn, and by their cell number, if they had any medical complaints. The warder recorded their replies, if any were forthcoming, in a notebook. When an examination, or treatment, was required the Nazi inmate was taken to the MI Room. A visit was usually completed in half an hour and the author was then able to proceed to the B.M.H. or back to his Regimental duties.

On a typical prison ward round the first call would be on Prisoner No. 1. In 1952 Baron Constantin von Neurath was suffering from cardiac failure and under treatment by an American Army cardiologist. Von Neurath was confined to bed in a converted office on the ground floor outside the main cellblock and the MO's daily visit was more in the nature of a courtesy call as demanded by the prison regulations. The Baron was an archetypal Prussian nobleman and had been Nazi ambassador in Britain in the 1930s. Hitler appointed him Gauleiter to Bohemia and Moravia in 1940. His influence on Hitler in instigating the Second World War and his actions against the Czech population in 1941, and early 1942, earned him a 15-year sentence at the Nuremberg War Crimes Tribunal. He was released early in 1955 on compassionate grounds having served only nine of his fifteen-year sentence.

With the exception of von Neurath and Prisoner No. 7, who spent most of his time in his cell, the other five Nazi war criminals were either outside in the exercising compound and gardening in their designated plots or sitting reading, writing and listening to music in the downstairs Common Room. Two Nazi naval officers, Grand Admiral Erich Raeder (No. 2) and Admiral Karl Doenitz (No. 3) were inseparable though there was some animosity between them. They were the only two high-ranking naval officers in Spandau and stood aloof from the other five political prisoners. Raeder was jealous because Doenitz had literally replaced him as one of Hitler's favourites in 1942. Known collectively as the 'Admiralty' to their fellow prisoners they were both medium-sized men and wore dark-blue naval overcoats and peaked caps even at the height of summer. The 'Admiralty' had no time for 'Rudolf Hess' and

Albert Speer, both of whom had, in their opinion, deserted the Nazi cause – 'Hess' by his desertion and flight to Britain in 1941 and Speer by his frank acknowledgement of the failings of the Nazi Party in relation to the Jewish holocaust and Concentration Camps. Though they seemed to present a solid front the 'Admiralty' nearly came to blows in January 1953. Raeder was inordinately proud of a giant turnip which he had laboriously, and lovingly, nurtured in the prison's vegetable garden through the harsh, wintry months of November and December 1952. The turnip had apparently reached its gargantuan size due to a long hot dry spring and lack of rain during the summer of 1952. One frosty night the turnip mysteriously vanished into thin air. Speer was suspected of the heinous offence and the only other dedicated gardener in Spandau was his 'Admiralty' colleague, Karl Doenitz. Raeder's rage lasted for three days and then died a natural death.

In contravention of the Geneva Convention Erich Raeder had been found guilty of signing an order to execute all captured Commandos following the Royal Naval Commando's successful raid on shipping in Bordeaux Harbour on the 7th of December 1942. In failing health Grand Admiral Raeder's life sentence was annulled on the 26th of September 1955 on compassionate grounds.

Prisoner No. 3, Admiral Karl Doenitz, had been awarded a ten-year sentence at Nuremberg for ordering his U-Boat commanders not to attempt saving the crews of torpedoed Allied shipping sunk in the Atlantic blockade. He served his ten-year sentence in full and was released from Spandau Prison in October 1956.

Prisoner No. 4, Walter Funk, was an enigma among the Nazi hierarchy at the prison. A short, pot-bellied, balding man, Funk had been a wealthy industrialist before he joined forces with the Nazi Party and became Hitler's Economics Minister and Director of the Reichsbank. He received a life sentence at Nuremberg for his direct orders to pilfer valuable art and jewellery from Jews and conquered races in Europe and, more incriminately, for ordering retrieval of gold dental implants from millions of victims who were murdered in German Concentration Camps. Prisoner No. 4 was a persistent whinger, ready at all times to complain about his unjust life sentence and a variety of medical symptoms. Funk suffered from "water trouble" and, once every quarter during the French duty month, a female accouchere dilated his urethra. Prisoner No 4 also became the central figure in an international incident during the French month in April 1953. An emergency committee was convened and a French surgeon announced dramatically that prisoner No. 4 was suffering from acute appendicitis and needed urgent surgery. The author's services at the B.M.H. were offered by the Commanding Officer, but the French and Russian delegates refused permission for Funk to be moved out of Spandau. As a compromise the prison chapel was converted into a temporary operating theatre. A French surgeon was lined up to perform the operation and the author's colleague at the B.M.H. was elected to deliver the anaesthetic. It took a whole week to set up the operation and, on the appointed day, the "little theatre" was jam-packed with observers from the Four Powers. When the B.M.H. anaesthetist, syringe in hand, advanced towards the prostrate patient on the operating table he noticed a rash on Funk's exposed abdomen and he immediately refused to carry on with the procedure. The operation was abandoned and pandemonium broke loose. Four Power colonels, majors and captains shouted at each other and the hapless Funk lay bewildered in the middle of the arguing mob. The eventual outcome was less dramatic. Without asking anyone's advice, or permission, a French surgeon carried out an appendectomy during their next monthly duty at Spandau in August. Whether the appendix was originally acutely inflamed, or showed evidence of previous inflammation after three months, was not recorded in Prisoner No. 4's medical notes.

Walter Funk tried his best to be on friendly terms with all his Nazi partners in crime. He was too self-centred to be accepted by them and they were fed up with his constant whingeing and tendency to burden them with the gross unfairness of his life sentence. The Admiralty avoided Funk like the plague. Albert Speer tolerated him up to a point and, depending on his mood, Hess would converse with No. 4 for a few minutes. Funk's only soul mate at Nuremberg and at Spandau was Baldur von Schirach, Prisoner No. 6, who was prepared to listen to his persistent whingeing with a sympathetic ear. Walter Funk's general health slowly deteriorated rapidly after his "famous" appendix operation. His life sentence was annulled and he was released from prison on compassionate grounds on the 16th May 1957 after only serving 11 years in captivity.

Prisoner No. 5, Albert Speer, proved to be the most charismatic Nazi of the seven sorry inmates at Spandau Prison. An architect by profession, Speer had wheedled his way into Adolf Hitler's favour in the mid-thirties by taking advantage of the Führer's grandiose vision for creating a Gothic-style empire centred on Berlin. Speer represented the cultural face of the Nazi hierarchy and was constantly at Hitler's side during visits from foreign dignitaries to the Reichschancellery in Berlin and at the Führer's Berghof, a mountain retreat in Bavaria. Speer was not officially appointed within the Nazi Party until 1943 when Hitler made him *Reichsminister* in charge of Armaments Production and, to satisfy demands from Germany's armed forces, he recruited thousands of foreign labourers from Detention and Concentration Camps. There is little doubt that his treatment of the conscripted labour force carried the death penalty at the Nuremberg Tribunal save for the fact he revealed in court that all top Nazis knew about the Concentration Camps and the Gas Chambers. As a result of these disclosures he was ostracised by his co-defendants at Nuremberg and most of his fellow inmates at Spandau considered he had only told the truth to save his own skin. He undoubtedly received a comparatively light sentence of 20 years considering he had been a top Nazi in Hitler's Third Reich and a close aide to the Führer throughout the 1930s and during World War II.

At Spandau Albert Speer felt sorry for Prisoner No. 7. He was aware at Nuremberg that "Hess" had a mental problem and his amnesia served to explain his failure to recall past events, in particular their collaboration in organising grand Party Rallies at Nuremberg. In Spandau there was more to it than amnesia. No. 7's feigned attacks of memory loss and depression led him to stay for days on end in his cell and he required assistance in cell-maintenance, laundry and personal hygiene. Speer did these chores on his behalf without complaint and urged "Hess" to join him in the exercise yard. When Speer was set free, having served his 20-year sentence on the 30th of December 1966, his concern for Prisoner No. 7 was exemplified by a request to the Prison Commissioners to release his cellmate on compassionate and humanitarian grounds. Conscious that No. 7 would now be the sole Nazi prisoner in Spandau he urged the authorities to take good care of "Hess" in his declining state of health.

In captivity Speer disciplined himself to a strict mental and physical regime and had a compulsive desire to keep fit. He exercised all day in the summer months and insisted on fighting his way around the compound in wintry weather. Speer was a stickler for statistics and estimated that, by the time he was released in December 1966, he had walked 24,000km, equivalent to the distance from Spandau to Mexico. He drafted two books while he was in prison and drew a series of architectural sketches for reconstructing war-torn Berlin. Having served a twenty-year sentence Albert Speer was released from Spandau on the 30th of December 1966 and 20 years later suffered a fatal stroke at a London hotel in September 1986.

Baldur von Schirach, Prisoner No. 6, was instrumental in establishing the Hitler Youth Movement in the 1930s and was gaoled for 20 years for his part in deporting 65,000 Jews from Vienna to Concentration Camps in Germany after Adolf Hitler made him Gauleiter of Austria in 1940. No. 6 was a stocky, grey-haired man with piercing, pale-blue eyes and evidently proud of his Aryan ancestry and a devoted dyed-in-the-wool Nazi. In 1952 and 1953 he had little time for Speer and "Hess" whom he regarded as deserters from his beloved Party. Curiously enough von Schirach later developed a rapport with Walter Funk and was prepared to listen to complaints about his ailments and unjust punishment. Von Schirach had no interest in gardening and, apart from some gentle exercising in the compound, his main occupation in captivity was reading and listening to music. By the time No. 6 was released, on the same day as Albert Speer, the 30th of December 1966, his eyesight was rapidly failing which makes one think his stiff, uncooperative manner and piercing stare might have been the result of his compromised vision and uncertainty about the author's military rank on his visits to the prison.

The author's first encounter with Prisoner No. 7 in Spandau occurred at 11.00am on the 2nd of May 1952. The prisoner, whom he took to be Rudolf Hess, was in his cell on the first floor of the detention block. When he entered with the warder, "Hess" was sitting under the grilled window reading a book. He immediately jumped to his feet. He was six inches taller than the author. The author approached "Hess" and inquired if he had any complaints. No. 7 transfixed him with a menacing stare from beneath his black, bushy eyebrows and made no effort to reply. They stood gazing awkwardly at each other for a full minute until the author broke the silence by requesting the warder to enter a plea of 'no complaints' in the register. The author glanced around the Spartan cell and noted that there were scraps of bread and stale food on the elevated, barred windowsill. After they departed, the warder explained No. 7 was going through a period of depression and was convinced the authorities, and Jews, were slowly poisoning him. The scraps of stale food on the window ledge were evidently kept as evidence he was being poisoned, should he see the end of his days in prison.

During 1952 and 1953 No. 7 was to be found on most days sitting alone in his cell reading books on Gothic history, philosophy and drama. He sometimes joined his fellow-prisoners in the Common Room but, even there, he tended to sit alone in the corner, reading or listening to the music of Wagner, Bach, Beethoven and Schubert, played on an ancient gramophone. Speer and Funk were the only two inmates who showed an interest in the reclusive, mentally unstable prisoner in their midst. To meet No. 7 outside in the exercise compound was a rare event. Wearing dark glasses, a leather flying jacket and peaked cap, Prisoner No. 7 strutted rapidly around the compound, totally ignored by the other prisoners and with a harassed warder trailing along behind in his wake. At a rough estimate Prisoner No.7 only replied to the "any complaints" query with a forceful *"Nein"* on a dozen occasions out of the forty or so 'ward-rounds' that the author conducted at Spandau Prison in 1952 and 1953.

Any minor complaints, such as headaches, coughs, sore throats, skin rashes and bowel disorders encountered on the daily rounds in Spandau were treated with prescribed medicines administered under strict control by the duty medical orderly. If an examination of one of the prisoners was required the patient was taken to the M.I. Room where minor surgery was also undertaken. The author syringed Grand Admiral Raeder's ears on two occasions to remove impacted wax. His naval companion, Admiral Karl Doenitz (No. 3), cut the back of his hand with a gardening tool and required an anti-tetanus injection and four stitches. Prisoner No. 4, Walter Funk, was a ready complainant but, when he found out he could get little change from the author, he kept his whingeing for the French duty month. Funk had found out over the years that the French warders and medical staff were sympathetic listeners to his complaints.

Prisoner No. 7 and Walter Funk caused more medical concern at Spandau than the other five Nazi inmates put together. "Hess's" mood swings were unpredictable and for days on end he would not speak to either the author or the Chief Warder. In a paranoid state on other days he sometimes complained his food was poisoned. Two negative forensic analyses of the scraps of food on his windowsill failed to convince him otherwise. When No. 7 decided on a few occasions to reply to the standard "Any complaints?" query he complained of headaches, dizziness and vomiting, none of which had a sound physical basis. Two aspirin tablets dissolved in warm water quickly resolved the situation. One snowbound night in January 1953, the author was ordered to make an emergency call to the prison at midnight. Prisoner No. 7 was creating a disturbance and preventing his cellmates from sleeping by shouting out in apparent agony and writhing on his bed. His cell was as cold as charity and the night warder wanted to transfer "Hess" to the M.I. Room. To move the patient on a stretcher to the ground floor would have been a major task and it was decided to examine No.7 in his dimly lit, ice-cold cell. He complained of a burning pain in the pit of his stomach and vomiting, though there was no evidence of the latter complaint. On examination the only positive clinical observation was tenderness above his navel. The author administered a generous morphine injection and the pain quickly subsided. Within ten minutes "Hess" was soundly asleep. During the routine visit the following day all his symptoms and signs had resolved and he was seated in the library reading a book.

Long before the January episode the author had come to a conclusion that Prisoner No. 7's complaints were mainly imagined. With his limited undergraduate training in psychiatry he had also arrived at a layman's diagnosis that Prisoner No. 7 was 'Bonkers.'

On the last Friday each month the Prison Commissioners held a luncheon involving the Four Powers. A medical officer and senior Guard Commander from each Power met with the warders and Prison Commandant to discuss in detail the medical condition of individual prisoners and to make suggestions to correct any complaints that arose. The Russian delegation made a meal of the occasion and turned up in numbers, one medical and one military colonel, their Prison M.O., an interpreter and two poker-faced civilians who took no part in the discussions and, in the author's opinion, were probably KGB agents. A perennial bone of contention at these conferences in 1952 and 1953 was the prisoners' weight loss during the Russian duty month, directly attributable to the Russian policy of adhering strictly to a dietary regime and orders to disturb the prisoners' sleep every two hours overnight. When challenged, the Russians played dumb and quoted rules laid down by the War Crimes Commissioners at Nuremberg. At the end of the meeting delegates were treated to a sumptuous feast, the Four Powers vying with each other in producing a culinary masterpiece. When the Russians were hosts all present approved of the quality of their vodka and the regularity of their toasts during the meal but this ploy only disguised the ordinary food served up. A prize for the best meals undoubtedly went to French chefs who delighted every-one with their cordon bleu cooking, providing unforgettable gastronomic experiences in post-war austerity days. The British and U.S. culinary efforts were firmly set somewhere in between basic Russian and haute cuisine French cooking.

The 1st Battalion Welsh Guards returned to the U.K in May 1953 for ceremonial duties at Queen Elizabeth II's coronation. The author was posted to an R.A.F Hospital at Rinteln where he served out the last four months of his National Service before returning home for demobilisation. During his time as Medical Officer to Spandau Prison there were no questions, or doubt, in his mind that the prisoner in Cell No. 7 was Rudolf Walter Richard Hess. His conversion to believe otherwise came in 1980 and speaks volumes for the uncanny acting ability of the impersonator at Spandau. The impostor convinced his colleagues, his guards, the prison authorities and his medical attendants, the author included, that he was truly Adolf Hitler's Deputy Führer in person. The author's close association with the "Spandau Seven" in 1952-53 led him to develop a keen interest in the fate of the seven Nazi prisoners and, in particular, the true identity of Prisoner No 7, and the mode of his death in Spandau's garden shed on 17th August 1987.

THE KAIZER OF ABERGAVENNY

Including a scattering of medieval castles, one of the many visitor attractions at the western end of the Welsh County of Monmouthshire, is a quaint 15th century parish church at Michaelstone-y-Fedw. The church is situated in the centre of a hamlet, ten miles equidistant from the cities of Newport and Cardiff, in southeast Wales. Two dozen, or so, private houses and a farmhouse are clustered around a central pub, The Cefn Mably Arms, and the adjacent church serves Michaelstone's parishioners. Within twenty yards of the lychgate, on the left side in the graveyard, there is a memorial stone dedicated to his wife by one Karl Hess from Schleswig in Germany. Scottish by birth, his wife, Elizabeth Mackie, was raised in Michaelstone-y-Fedw. Karl was employed as a steward to the Bishop of Gloucester in 1889 and Elizabeth was a housemaid in the same establishment. They married in 1890 and settled down at Exmouth in Devon. Their blissful union was short-lived and, a year later, Elizabeth tragically died of pneumonia. Karl arranged for his wife's body to be interred at the parish churchyard of her former home. The gravestone records her death on the 13th of June 1891, aged 35 years, and is inscribed 'In life beloved. In death never forgotten'.

After his wife's premature demise, Karl Hess returned to the bosom of his extended family in Schleswig on the German-Danish border and, within two years, he remarried. Contrary to popular belief, Karl Hess, whom Rudolf called 'uncle', was his father's first cousin. The Hess family in Schleswig were a powerful, closely knit group and by the time Rudolf was old enough to understand family connections he would have been made aware that Uncle Karl Hess's first wife, who had died three years before he was born, was buried 'somewhere near Cardiff in South Wales'. Rudolf Hess had no inkling at the time that he would, one day, end up at a hospital near Abergavenny and within spitting distance of Michaelstone-y-Fedw.

Adolf Hitler's Deputy Führer flew solo in a Messerschmitt 110, twin-engine fighter, from Augsburg in Bavaria to Scotland and parachuted to the ground 16 miles south of Glasgow on the May 10th, 1941. Rudolf Hess was ostensibly on a peace mission but was immediately arrested and spent his first night in captivity at Maryhill Barracks in Glasgow. During the next four days he was held under guard at Buchanan Castle and, by order of Winston Churchill, he was transferred to the Tower of London, the implication being that, if it was proven he was spying, he would be summarily executed. After five days in the Tower Hess was re-classified as an officer prisoner-of-war and taken to Mytchett Place in Aldershot. Closely guarded, and under constant interrogation, he was imprisoned at Mytchett Place for fourteen months and, during this period his movements outside the detention centre were severely restricted. Finally, in July 1942, the Nazi celebrity P.O.W. was relocated to Maindiff Court Hospital, Abergavenny, where he remained for three and a half years and was known to the locals as 'The Kaiser'.

In October 1945 the prisoner held at Maindiff Court Hospital was flown to Nuremberg, one of twenty-three 'top' Nazis to stand trial for their war crimes. Robert Ley committed suicide before proceedings began and the remaining twenty-two were sentenced on the 1st of October 1946 after a trial lasting eleven months. Three Nazis were acquitted and twelve were sentenced to death by hanging, but Hermann Göering cheated the gallows by taking cyanide in his cell two hours before he was due to be executed. The remaining seven were sent to Spandau Prison in Berlin for varying periods of confinement. The "Kaiser of Abergavenny" was sentenced to life imprisonment and in his case it literally meant life. Known as Prisoner No. 7 in Spandau the one-time Nazi supremo took his own life on August 20th,1987, at the age of 93 years, having spent five years short of half a century in prison.

One authoritative writer has advanced a theory that the "Kaiser of Abergavenny" was an impostor who had flown from Germany to Scotland in the place of Rudolf Hess and the Deputy Führer's plane was dispatched by the Luftwaffe over the North Sea. Two compelling pointers discount this theory as an extremely remote possibility. The first improbability is that Rudolf Hess's look-alike would not have had the competence to fly a Messerschmitt 110 fighter for close to 800 miles from Denmark to within twelve miles of its targeted destination on the west coast of Scotland. Hess himself was a competent aviator and an expert navigator. Secondly, during his incarceration at Maindiff Court Hospital, Hess made repeated requests to be allowed to visit his Uncle Karl's first wife's grave at Michaelstone-y-Fedw, only 30 miles distant from the hospital. He was refused permission on every occasion. However well-prepared the impostor might have been in Germany before the flight it is impossible to imagine he would have been told about Elizabeth Hess's grave at a remote churchyard in rural Wales. On the basis of these pointers there can be little doubt that the important Nazi prisoner held at Maindiff Court Hospital was none other than Germany's Deputy Führer, Walter Rudolph Richard Hess.

Whether Prisoner No. 7 in Spandau was the "true" Hess has been challenged by a few speculative writers, including Dr R Hugh Thomas in his two publications "The Murder of Rudolf Hess" in 1979, and "A Tale of Two Murders" in 1988. On two occasions in 1973 Dr Thomas had had the opportunity to examine 'Hess' when he was referred to the British Military Hospital in Berlin for X-Rays. A military specialist surgeon at the B.M.H., Thomas found no evidence of scarring on Prisoner No. 7's chest wall, a legacy of a penetrating gunshot wound Hess sustained in Romania in August 1917 during World War I. As a result he was hospitalized for three months and only returned to active duty in March 1918. In view of the severity of the trauma, the bullet entry and exit sites would almost certainly leave life-long scars on Hess's chest wall. Observation by a highly trained clinical surgeon, and negative recording of the relevant scars at two post-mortem examinations performed after the prisoner's death, serve to pinpoint that the Nazi in Spandau was not Rudolf Hess but an impostor, similar to the Deputy Führer in appearance, speech and mannerisms.

During National Service in Berlin in 1952 and 1953 the author served as Regimental Medical Officer to the Welsh Guards, and part of his duties was to visit Spandau Prison during each of the three months when the Guards took over custody of the prison. His rank at the time was Captain in the R.A.M.C, the Royal Army Medical Corps, and he was required to make contact with the prisoners every day during the duty months. In 1952 there were seven notorious Nazi war criminals at Spandau including Prisoner No. 7, supposedly Rudolf Hess. At the time he had no reason to suspect the man in cell No. 7 was an impostor. In recent years, however he has become dubious about "Hess's" identity and eventually became convinced that the man who underwent assisted euthanasia at Spandau in August 1987, was a faker. What became of the 'real' Hess is an enigma, which will remain an object for speculation and conjecture, and it forms the basis of the fictional content of this novel.

The truth may never see the light of day. It may be revealed by the eventual disclosure of secret files on the subject still held somewhere in the bowels of the Foreign Office or in MI5 and MI6 archives. Should the author's conjecture about the contents of these files prove to be incorrect, and the prisoner he attended in 1952 and 1953 at Spandau was the real McCoy, he would be the first to admit his errors of judgement. He shall, however, still rest content in the knowledge he has contributed a readable account of the conspiracy surrounding the ultimate fate of Adolf Hitler's Deputy Führer.

RUDOLF HESS – A BIOGRAPHY

Rudolf Hess was born on the 26th of April 1894 at Alexandria in Egypt. His father, Fritz Hess, and Klara Münch, his newlywed 25-year-old wife from Hof in Franconia, arrived at Alexandria in 1890 to run a hugely successful import-export business at the Docks. After completion of the Suez Canal in 1869 Alexandria had become a major commercial trading port and a lucrative source of income for Fritz Hess's company. Consequently the Hess family's first infant was born into a rich, middle-class fraternity. They lived in a three-storey villa in the wealthy Ibrahimieh suburb of the city, only 200 metres from the Mediterranean shoreline. The villa was surrounded by sub-tropical gardens, cultivated by an Egyptian ghaffer. Klara Hess cleaned the house, cooked and educated her young infant only employing a nursemaid when Rudolf was a toddler. She was well-educated, religious, tender-hearted and extremely musical -- in contrast to her husband who presented a dual personality, one at work and the other at his palatial home, his replica Bavarian castle, at Ibrahimieh.

At Hess and Co.'s import-export offices in Alexandria docks Fritz Hess was highly respected by his British and French counterparts and had a reputation for politeness and fair-dealing. In the privacy of his home, however, he became a stern and bigoted man and ran his household like a feudal, Prussian baronial castle. Meals had to be served at set times and the family had to congregate at the dining table to await the master's arrival. Silence was strictly observed during mealtimes unless conversation was initiated by the master of the house. Rudolf was expected to appear punctually, neatly dressed with combed hair and scrubbed hands. Bedtimes were strictly observed. Rudolf was only allowed to play with his toys when his father was out of the house. He was also forbidden to show any affection towards his father, which was regarded as a sign of weakness, and his childhood was overshadowed by fear of his dictatorial male parent. As a result he grew into a withdrawn and repressed child, lacking self-confidence and crying out for paternal affection. Despite all these strictures Rudolf admired, and was proud of, his father's achievements in life and, for his part, Fritz Hess was determined to groom his eldest son to follow in his footsteps into the successful family import-export business, Hess and Co. of Alexandria. Rudolf loved his mother though she dutifully supported her husband's autocratic behaviour, maintaining it was normal in families of their standing in Prussia and Bavaria. Klara Hess unsuccessfully attempted teaching Rudolf to play the piano and, as he grew up, encouraged his interest in astrology and archaeology. She also made certain that the apple of her eye had a mechanical railway set, a motor car, lead soldiers of the Franco-Prussian war and a rudimentary airship and aeroplane as play-things.

At six years of age Rudolf attended a German Protestant school in Alexandria for only one term. Up to this point his mother had tutored him at home and thereafter he received private tuition in the family house at Ibrahimieh. One teacher stood head and shoulders above all others. Abd-al-Aziz Effendi was a cultured and talented Don who taught Rudolf basic Arabic, English and French and the main stress was on German history and literature, both strongly approved of by his Teutonic father who idolized the German emperor, Kaiser Wilhelm.

Rudolf's brother, Albert, was born in 1897 and his sister, Charlotte, in 1908. Fritz Hess had inherited a large family house at Reicholdsgrün in the Bavarian, Fitchel Mountains and, during the hottest Egyptian months of July and August, the Hess family travelled en-bloc from Alexandria to their German mountain retreat. These summer pilgrimages continued until the outbreak of World War I when Hess and Co. was shut down by the Allies. In Egypt Rudolf never achieved his childhood ambition of visiting the many ancient sites and monuments which abound in North Africa. Accompanied by his mother and Abd-al-Aziz Effendi he was taken by train from Alexandria to Cairo and stayed for one night at Mena House Hotel near the pyramids. The wondrous sights he saw in Cairo remained in Rudolf's memory for the rest of his life.

In March 1908, when Rudolf was 14 years of age, his father enrolled him at a Lutheran Protestant boarding school at Godesberg-am-Rhein and, after 3 years, he graduated in mathematics, physics and chemistry. The teaching staff at the boarding school were convinced he had potential to become a scientist but Fritz Hess thought otherwise. At Godesberg-am-Rhein Rudolf was shunned by his peers who labelled him 'The Egyptian' due to his swarthy complexion and 'deep-set', doleful eyes. He had grown into a tall, good-looking, gangly teenager with a dreamy-eyed face and he neither drank alcohol nor smoked. He rarely smiled. In Egypt the principles of German nationalism had been regularly drummed into him by his father. At boarding school he strived to erase his Egyptian past and became more nationalistic than any of his fellow pupils. As a consequence Rudolf developed into an introspective loner with no male friends at Godesberg-am-Rhein and no interest in the opposite sex.

In accordance with his father's wishes Rudolf left the boarding school in the summer of 1911 to enrol at a Swiss commercial college at Neuchatel, thus ending his dream of becoming a physicist or an astronomer. He was completely disinterested in the world of commerce and made little effort to hide his displeasure. He withdrew further into his shell, becoming introspective and moody, and started exhibiting signs of depression, which was to plague him throughout his adult life.

In 1914 Germany was a wealthy, rapidly expanding nation of 68 million people with a large army and navy. Hankering for further expansion eastwards it formed a Triple Alliance with

Austria-Hungary and Italy. To counteract Kaiser Wilhelm's intention in this direction Britain and France united in a Triple Entente with Russia and the foundations for a European conflict were laid. Germany declared war on Russia and France and Britain responded on the third and fourth of August 1914. At the outbreak of World War I Rudolf Hess was undertaking a commercial apprenticeship with a shipping company in Hamburg. He saw his way out of his dilemma in commerce and for the first time in his life, at twenty years of age, Rudolf disobeyed his father and volunteered to join the German army. He enlisted in the Seventh Bavarian Field Artillery Regiment at Munich on the 20th of August 1914 and, a month later, transferred to the First Bavarian König Infantry Regiment. By November 4th his regiment was in the front line at Ypres on the Western Front. Fighting on the ground, at that time, was mobile and the horrors of trench warfare were yet to come. Hess suffered minor leg wounds from shrapnel in a futile attack on Britain's Expeditionary Force veterans at Langemark. He was awarded an Iron Cross (2nd Class) for bravery. For the next seven months he fought in the trenches on the Somme battlefields. Promoted corporal, Hess was transferred to the Verdun salient in the spring of 1916 and, on the 12th of June, he again suffered shrapnel wounds to his legs and back at Duamont. In hospital Hess read about Richthofen's Flying Circus and applied to join the German Imperial Air Corps. He was rejected.

Promoted sergeant in charge of No.10 Company Bavarian Reserve Infantry Hess was posted to Romania on the Eastern Front in January 1917. In a skirmish on the 23rd of July he received injuries from shell splinters to his left arm and hand, and was treated at a Casualty Clearing Station. On returning to his Unit he was involved in a battle at Focsani on the 8th of August, sustaining a close-range gunshot wound to his left chest. The bullet entered from below his left armpit and exited at the back under his left shoulder blade. Evacuated from the battlefield Hess was treated in Hungarian and German hospitals and eventually sent home to Reicholdsgrün to recuperate on the 11th of December 1917. While still in hospital he received his commission as an infantry Lieutenant and again applied to the Air Corps for pilot training. His second request was accepted. Hess commenced his flying instruction in a Fokker D VII training aircraft on the 15th March 1918 and had completed his course as a pilot by the 4th of October. Lieutenant Rudolf Hess was on aerial combat duty for only one month before an armistice was declared on the 11th of November 1918. By Christmas 1918, Bavarian Fighter Squadron Jagdstaffel 35(b) had been disbanded and Rudolf Hess was discharged from military service on 13th of December. He now retired to Reicholdsgrün to lick his wounds and ponder why Germany had lost the war.

MUNICH AND THE NAZI PARTY

JANUARY 1919- MAY 1941

Throughout 1919 Hess lived with his family at Reicholdsgrün, brooding over the fate of his beloved Fatherland and planning his future. Fritz Hess and his family were now living permanently at Reicholdsgrün, his import-export business in Alexandria having been expropriated by the British in 1914. Consequently there was no business inheritance for Rudolf and continued military service was not an option and prohibited by the Treaty of Versailles. Encouraged by his father, 26-year-old Rudolf enlisted as a mature political and economic student at Munich University in February 1920.

At the University Hess came under the tutelage of the Professor of Geopolitics. A retired pre-war army general, Professor Karl Haushofer took Rudolf under his wing and his son, 18-year-old Albrecht, was in the same study group. Professor Haushofer was a dynamic tutor and entertained strong political views on National Socialism, Bolshevism, Judaism and lebensraum for the German *herrenvolk*. He tended to run with the hare and hounds and used his pupils to propagate his political theories without his personal involvement. In Rudolf Hess he found a willing horse. Prompted by the professor Rudolf had enlisted in a company of Frei Corps Epp Stormtroopers in May 1919, and in February 1920, he became a member of the Thule Society, a clandestine anti-Bolshevik, anti-Judaism organisation practising mystical and occult rituals. The Society met secretly and used astronomy predictions as part of their meetings, mainly concerned with the evils of Communism and Judaism. Professor Haushofer also introduced Rudolf at one of Adolf Hitler's earliest meetings at a Munich beer hall on the 21st of February 1920.

Despite his farcical appearance, his music-hall moustache and his down-at-heel attire, Adolf Hitler was a mesmerising speaker advocating unemployed Germans to form a united party which he proposed should be called The National Socialist German Workers Party, a precursor of the Nazi Party. Rudolf enrolled as member No.16 in June of that year and thereafter attended most of Hitler's speaking engagements, usually taking on the duty of introducing the Führer and keeping records of the meetings. Hitler's lengthy speeches were centred around the unjust terms of the Treaty of Versailles, the influence of Jews on German economy, the serious threat of Bolshevism and the German government's inability to deal with unemployment which affected almost everyone present at the Party's weekly gatherings. He promised work and prosperity for all, and everyone, if they united and joined his Party of National Socialism. At a *bierhalle* punch-up in Munich on 4th November 1921, a tankard was hurled from the crowd, aimed at Adolf Hitler. The missile struck Hess on his temple leaving a permanent scar. Allegedly designed by Rudolf Hess, the Swastika was adopted as the Party's official emblem in the summer of 1923.

The main opposition to Hitler's fledgling Party were the Red Bolsheviks in Munich, Berlin, and Northern German cities. Hitler's Party required muscle power and, in 1921, the *Sturm Abteilung* (SA) were recruited as an elitist cadre of a thousand veteran storm troopers from World War I and from the disbanded Frei Corps Epp. An arrogant, homosexual, ex-Army officer called Ernst Röhm became a Party member in 1921 and made himself commander of the SA, or Brownshirts, as they were popularly called. Röhm's objective was elimination of the Bolshevik Party in Bavaria and Southern Germany and, within two years, this had been achieved. The Communist threat, however, still thrived in Berlin and Northern German cities and this fact, and the Weimar Republic's inability to respond to French reoccupation of the industrial Ruhr in 1923, convinced Hitler that the political powerhouse in Berlin needed to be replaced. In the autumn of 1923 Hitler was urging Ernst Röhm's Brownshirts to march on Berlin and he declared a National Revolution which became known as The Beer Hall Putsch.

The Putsch occurred in Munich over two days, 8th and 9th of November, 1923. Brandishing a pistol, and with Rudolf Hess at his side, Hitler stormed the Bürgerbraükeller in Munich where Bavarian government officials were conducting a public meeting on the night of November 8th. Firing a shot into the ceiling Hitler advanced to the platform and forced the Chairman, Gustav Khar, to step aside. The Führer then made an impassioned speech convincing the two thousand delegates present to join his Party. Rudolf Hess drove the deposed officials to a safe house in the suburbs of Munich. Next day, 9th November, Rudolf's student SA Company stormed the City Hall and hoisted a Swastika flag. At the same time Hitler and General Ludendorf led the insurgents on a peaceful march to Munich's city centre. The parade was abandoned in panic when Weimar government troops and police opened fire, wounding several Nazis including Hermann Göering, a Munich University student at the time and a supporter of Hitler's newly formed Party. Adolf Hitler fled the scene and sought refuge in Karl

Haushofer's villa at Staffelsee. Three days after the Putsch, Hitler was arrested. Hess heard the Putsch had failed and dashed to safety across the border to Salzburg in Austria. Hitler received a five-year sentence for his part in the Munich Beer Hall Putsch and was sent to Landsberg Prison on 1st April 1924. By that time Rudolf Hess could no longer survive being separated from his beloved Führer. He gave himself up to the German authorities and, in May 1924, he also was sent to Landsberg for eighteen months for his involvement in the Putsch. Rudolf was again a happy man to be reunited at Landsberg Prison with his idol and inspirational father figure.

Prison life was not taxing for the Nazi National Socialists. They lived in comfort in adjacent cells and, during their nine months together, they collaborated in writing Hitler's magnum opus, *Mein Kampf*. By now Hess was closer to Hitler than any Party member and, in public, the Führer only referred to Rudolf Hess and Ernst Röhm with the possessive pronoun 'Du'. Professor Karl Haushofer was a regular visitor at Landsberg Prison and he persuaded Hitler to abandon military action, which might culminate in a civil war, advising instead a political solution to attaining power in Germany's bankrupt state. Another frequent visitor at Landsberg was twenty-two year old Ilse Pröhl. Daughter of a Berlin army physician; Ilse enrolled as a philosophy student at Munich University in 1920 and became friendly with Rudolf Hess. She admired Adolf Hitler's ideals and visions for a greater Germany and his aims to acquire 'Lebensraum' at the expense of Slavic nations. Ilse never became a Party member but took an active role in broadcasting the arrival of Hitler's Nazi Party and helping Hess to disseminate Party propaganda throughout Germany. Adolf Hitler was granted an early release from Landsberg on 20th

December 1924 and Rudolf Hess was set free ten days later. On each occasion Ilse Pröhl drove the pardoned prisoners into Munich and freedom.

In February 1925, and in the presence of 4,000 followers, Adolf Hitler formally registered his Nazi Party as a political organisation and, in 1926, he created the *Schutzstaffel*, or S.S, to become his private protection force. In the same year he appointed Rudolf Hess as his private secretary. Rudolf's soft, sensitive nature and his cloying tenderness towards the Führer led to references by Party loyalists to "Fräulein Hess". He counteracted this impression by behaving with exaggerated masculinity and strutted around in a manly fashion in his SA, or SS, uniform. He would do anything for the Führer though the act might put a strain on his sense of decency, or honour, as might befit a British aristocrat whom he strove to emulate. Adolf Hitler's prompting made Hess propose to Ilse Pröhl and they were married at a civil ceremony in Munich on 20th December 1927. Professor Karl Haushofer and Adolf Hitler were witnesses at the ceremony and Rudolf and his new bride were provided with a sumptuous villa in the Harlaching district of Munich. Ilse and Rudolf Hess had a happy marital life together and their union was eventually blessed by the birth of their only son in 1937, ten years after they were married. The boy was christened Wolf Rüdiger Adolf Karl Hess, the latter two forenames in acknowledgment of the Führer and Professor Karl Haushofer, his one-time teacher and mentor at Munich University.

In his early thirties, Rudolf Hess was slender in build with a tall frame and over six feet in height. He had an angular face crowned by centrally parted black hair, a prominent over-hanging forehead, black, bushy eyebrows, greyish-green eyes and a solid, square chin. He was completely humourless and, as an organizer, indecisive and ready to delegate tasks to his subordinates. He took pride in his dress and his favoured uniform was a black SS tunic with a Colonel's badges of rank and a flaming red Swastika armband. For recreation he enjoyed fast motoring in his brown Mercedes Benz Coupe and flying his private plane. He and Ilse were keen on mountaineering and skiing in the German and Austrian Alpine resorts.

In 1927, with money provided by the industrialist, Baron von Thyssen, a completely refurbished Braunhaus became the Nazi Party headquarters in Munich. Rudolf was made Gauleiter and given a capacious suite and his personal secretariat. Martin Bormann was appointed his private secretary and, for a few years, Heinrich Himmler and Joseph Göebbels were under the same roof, the former in charge of the secret police and the SS, Hitler's private bodyguard, and the latter responsible for Party propaganda and editor of a weekly newssheet, The *Volkisher Beobachter*. By 1928 Berlin was the epicentre for political power in Germany. The Nazi Party was actively striving to become a credible political force and Adolf Hitler moved his power-base to Berlin and, in Munich, Rudolf Hess was content to stand aside and allow Bormann, Himmler and Göebbels to run the Party's affairs. Never himself power-hungry, he was content to remain the Führer's closest confidant and confederate. For this purpose Hess was provided with a modest apartment in Berlin and commuted from Munich by air, often flying his own two-seater monoplane supplied by industrialist benefactors of the Nazi Party.

Between 1930 and 1934 Rudolf Hess was at the zenith of his power within the Nazi Party. His major contributions were in formulating Party rules and recruiting German residents abroad to support and enrol in the Nazi Party. He was fanatically devoted to Hitler and his uncompromising loyalty kept him his place within the Party hierarchy. Constantly at the Führer's side he controlled Hitler's political and military engagements and took care to ensure his idol's speeches were not exposed to contradictory interventions by arranging handpicked audiences.

The democratically elected Weimar Parliament of February 1932 in Berlin failed to function. The Nazi Party held 230 seats but was outvoted by an extremist Marxist element in the Reichstag. Hitler threatened to alert Ernst Röhm's 400,000 SA troopers to deal with the Communist insurgents and a second election was convened later that year in November 1932. The Nazi Party secured a majority and, on January 30th, 1933, Hitler was made Chancellor by President Hindenburg. As Cabinet Minister without Portfolio in the newly elected Parliament, Hess was responsible for introducing an Enabling Act, which allowed Adolf Hitler eventually to become President of Germany. On 2nd August 1934 the acting Weimar President, von Hindenburg, died and Hitler elected himself to replace him. Germany now ceased to be a democracy and became a dictatorship under iron-rod control by a powerful demagogue.

The Führer's first appointment as Chancellor was to make Rudolf Hess his successor and Deputy Führer. Other Party appointments   followed.   Hermann   Göering   became Reichspresident, and Prime Minister of Prussia with an army of one thousand stormtroopers; Joseph Göebbels was in charge of Party propaganda and controlled all radio stations and owned the newspaper, *Volkischer Beobachter*. Ernst Röhm's 400,000 Brownshirts were the Party's muscle power, and Heinrich Himmler commanded Hitler's 1,000-strong SS battalion and the Third Reich's secret police -- later to become the Gestapo.

Martin Bormann was elected to become Hitler's private secretary, thus relieving Hess of his immediate obligations to the Führer. Hess's interest in foreign affairs was thwarted when Joachim von Ribbentrop came on the scene in 1934 and insisted on becoming Ambassador to Great Britain in 1936. Most of these top-ranking Nazis were hungry for ultimate control of the Party but Rudolf Hess was the exception. He was content to sit back on the sidelines, basking in his master's reflected glory and, in his opinion, being steadfastly loyal to the greatest German that ever walked the earth, Germany's saviour after the Great War and guiding light for a glorious future in his Third Reich dictatorship.

Within the Party itself there were those who doubted Hess's sanity, his ability to make important decisions, his limited political insight and his suitability to hold high office. The Führer would not tolerate any derogatory remarks about his Deputy whom he treated like a brother. These doubts about Hess's political capabilities were not without foundation, in particular his mental state. When the Nazi Party emerged on the political scene in Berlin in 1930 Hess started complaining of psychosomatic illnesses - digestive disorders, stomach cramps, kidney and pericardiac pains and insomnia. To Hess these symptoms were not imagined but real and, finding little benefit from conventional medical therapies, he turned to alternative treatments prescribed by homeopathic practitioners and faith healers. His favourite holistic guru in Munich was Pastor Kreipp who convinced Rudolf he should become a strict vegetarian and he became a slave to out-of-the-way health cures prescribed by the quack Pastor. At his office in the Braunhaus he was polite and formal to his staff but subject to bouts of suppressed anger ending up with stomach cramps, a condition referred to by psychotherapists as a 'hysterical escape syndrome.' As a cure for his paranoia Hess soon developed an interest in clairvoyance and divining rods in search of underground health-giving water sources.

Hess's elevation to Deputy Führer relieved him from most of his Party obligations but allowed him to sit in at all important committees, which bolstered his ego and sense of self-importance. Adolf Hitler was content with this arrangement in the knowledge that Hess would support all his decisions, come Hell and high water, and sign decrees and laws on his behalf without question. Rudolf was also groomed to be the acceptable face of the Nazi Party and was encouraged to continue his contacts with foreign diplomats and German citizens living abroad.

Hermann Göering came from a wealthy background and had a distinguished career as a fighter pilot in the 1914-1918 conflict. He ended the war as commandant of Richthofen's Flying Circus with 22 Allied 'kills' to his credit. In the early 1920s Göering was a student at Munich University. Uninterested in National Socialism *per se*, and as a diversion from boredom, he flirted with the Nazis and was wounded in the Beer Hall Putsch in November 1923. He then disappeared from the German political scene and, for three years after his wife's death, lived in Sweden. Returning to German politics in 1927 he saw the potential of the Nazi Party and fostered an ambition to replace Adolf Hitler as its leader. A charismatic personality with a brilliant war record and much loved by the German nation, Göering was immediately embraced by Adolf Hitler and, by the mid-1930s, he had supplanted Hess as the Party's showpiece. Whereas photographs at Party functions and military parades prior to 1937 had shown Rudolf Hess standing at the Führer's right hand, subsequent photos nearly always had a uniformed, corpulent, smiling Hermann Göering accompanying the Führer and wielding an Air Marshal's baton, like the conductor of an orchestra. Hess felt his demotion from Hitler's favour acutely but, being a 'gentleman' with a stiff upper lip, he showed no outward emotion or hostility towards Hermann Göering. Rather, he resorted to his imagined psychosomatic problems and suffered in silence.

Adolf Hitler's objectives in 1934 were fourfold. Firstly, he aimed to overturn the stringent reparations Germany had to pay as a result of the Treaty of Versailles; secondly, he wished to pass laws to order able-bodied men to rebuild industrial Germany and the autobahns, thus resolving mass unemployment during the World depression; thirdly, he had visions of a pure, blonde, blue-eyed Aryan race and advocated voluntary, or forcible, deportation of Jews, Romanys and citizens of Slavic origin and fourthly, he needed lebensraum to increase the land area available to his expanding Aryan nation. With this in mind the Chancellor fixed his gaze on the Eastern Europe states and, to achieve his aim, he was prepared to expand his army and navy and to eliminate Bolshevism off the face of the earth. Rudolf Hess was a devotee of all these grandiose aims and Adolf Hitler could count on his full support in their implementation.

A major test for the infant dictatorship came in January 1934. Adolf demanded unqualified support from the Reichswher, the official German army of 100,000 men as decreed by the Treaty of Versailles. The generals would not support the Nazis as long as Ernst Röhm had ambitions to become supreme commander of all German armed forces. The Reichswher generals persuaded Hitler to disband the Brownshirts. In June 1934, in a coup titled

'The Night of the Long Knives', Adolf Hitler led a group of SS officers to an hotel on the Tegensee where Röhm and a group of homosexual officers were spending a fortnight's leave. They were all arrested and taken to Stadelheim Prison where they were summarily executed. Hermann Göering's storm troopers and Himmler's SS made simultaneous arrests at the SA's main barracks in Berlin and Hamburg. The Nazi Party's strong arm since the very beginning, the Brownshirt SA were virtually wiped out overnight and 83 SA executive officers met their deaths on the 'Night of the Long Knives'. Most of the SA storm troopers re-enlisted in the Reichswher and re-classified as the Wehrmacht in the following year. All Wehrmacht officers and men had to swear an oath of allegiance to the Führer, Adolf Hitler. Rudolf Hess had no prior knowledge of the coup and, though his conscience abhorred the executions -- a Lieutenant Schneidhuber, Hess's adjutant at the Braunhaus, was one of the victims -- as a loyal yes-man he supported the Führer's actions in public.

To celebrate Adolf Hitler's accession to ultimate power, Hess arranged a party rally at Nuremberg on the 10th of September 1934. The Deputy introduced the Führer to the crowds and massed Wehrmacht and SS troops ending his introduction with the words – "Germany will live because our Führer, Adolf Hitler, lives. Heil Hitler." Rudolf was a poor speaker. Nervous, uninspiring and sometimes incoherent, his speeches were punctuated by embarrassing pauses. Hitler, on the other hand, mesmerized audiences and decreed the Rally should become an annual event. The following year Albert Speer, Hess's protégé and a qualified architect, assisted in planning and decorating the rostrum with hundreds of Swastika flags. Held at the Zeppelin Fields, an open-air auditorium in Nuremberg, the

Rally was a huge success and became a spectacular annual event until the outbreak of World War II in 1939.

Hess took the main credit for the Rally and introduced the Führer each year but arrangements were mainly delegated to Albert Speer and Joseph Göebbels. Adolf Hitler was fanatical about architecture and had grandiose plans for re-building a Gothic citadel in the centre of Berlin as a permanent memorial to his glorious one-thousand-year Third Reich. In his visionary fantasies he spent hours in the Reichschancellery in the company of Albert Speer, drooling over scale models of buildings and highways. Within a year, and much to Hess's annoyance, Speer became a constant fixture in the Führer's entourage both in Berlin and at the Berghof, Hitler's mountain retreat at Berchtesgaden in Bavaria.

In his capacity as Deputy Führer Rudolf Hess was signatory to many important Party decrees on behalf of the Führer. On the 10th of September 1935 he signed the Nuremberg Laws, a programme for religious and racial persecution of Jews and other non-Aryan citizens who would be subjected to deportation from Germany. By 1938 battalions of Waffen SS had been recruited to deal with this problem and Hess asserted at the time – "They, that is the Waffen SS, are specifically trained in racial matters." Hess was given an honorary rank of Colonel-General in the SS in 1936 and their black uniforms with a red Swastika armband became his favoured uniform at military functions. In October 1934 Hess formed a Foreign Affairs Department to monitor German embassies abroad and to supervise the interests of German citizens living outside the Third Reich. On the 16th of March 1935, as a member of the Reich's Defence Council, he signed a Conscription Law in defiance of the League of Nations and made himself responsible for administrating the economic and political preparations for any conflict involving the Third Reich.

By the end of 1937 Rudolf's intimate association with Adolf Hitler steadily declined due to the Führer's greater involvement in military matters. Hitler had constant battles with Wehrmacht generals and Hess could not tolerate the stiff, autocratic Prussian officers who regarded him as a backward lightweight and the Führer's fawning stool pigeon. Even Hermann Göering called him a 'piesil', a boring, unimaginative, awestruck Cadet. Joachim von Ribbentrop took over Foreign Affairs from Hess in 1936. He had been Germany's ambassador in London and a confidant of Edward VIII during his abdication crisis in December. Von Ribbentrop was on friendly terms with the King of England and, according to Embassy sources, on even friendlier terms with Mrs Wallis-Simpson, King Edward VIII's twice-divorced partner. On his return to Germany the Führer made von Ribbentrop Germany's Foreign Minister, which left Rudolf Hess's interests abroad confined to running the Auslands Organization, regarded as potentially useful in the event of any future conflict involving Germany.

Between 1934 and the outbreak of World War II, the Führer used Göering and Hess as Party showpieces to entertain foreign dignitaries. A tall, fairly good-looking man resplendent in his black SS Colonel's uniform, Rudolf presented a stately, military image. He was polite and courteous to visitors but lacking in charisma and the impression he gave was of a cold fish with piercing, grey-green eyes sheltering under black, bushy eyebrows. His involvement in conversation was restricted to ordinary platitudes. These negative attributes were not helped by his peculiar dietary habits and his proneness to succumb to psychosomatic illnesses. Hovering in the background, Rudolf

Hess was present to meet and greet many of Hitler's important guests at the Chancellery, or the Berghof. He would be called forwards to be introduced to the visitors and formally address them with a stiff, exaggerated Nazi salute embellished with clicking of his heels. He then retired to the background and took no part in any discussions unless invited to do so by the Führer. Any contributions he made were usually to repeat the Führer's comments. The same applied in military councils where, in the presence of high-ranking officers, the Deputy Führer felt uncomfortable and he either took to staring into space in stony silence, or his stomach, or chest pains, forced him to excuse himself and retire from the Council Chamber. Reichsmarshall Göering, on the other hand, gave as good as he got and he bullied his military counterparts, thereby gaining ground in the Führer's estimation. So much so that, by 1938, Göering had supplanted Hess in the Führer's inner circle and virtually became Adolf Hitler's deputy. Despite his demotion Hess remained a staunch believer in Adolf Hitler and his plans and visions for a greater Germany with a leading place among the nations of the world.

During the six years of his Deputy Führership, Hess rubbed shoulders with most European leaders of the day -- presidents, ministers, ambassadors, diplomats and military officials. His personal foreign affairs advisors, Professor Karl Haushofer and Haushofer's son, Albrecht, had established contacts with Prime Minister Stanley Baldwin and Rab Butler in Britain and, through their good auspices, Hess's department had a foothold in the British government. Headed by the Foreign Minister, Anthony Eden, a British all-Party delegation paid a visit to Berlin in 1935. Foreign Minister Eden was cool and unbending, but World War I Prime Minister, David Lloyd George, professed his admiration for the Führer's achievements since coming to power. At the Olympic Games in Berlin in August 1936 Adolf Hitler attended the opening and closing ceremonies and on the final day witnessed Jesse Owens, a black American athlete, breaking the world sprint record and securing four Olympic gold medals, much to the embarrassment of the Nazi hierarchy. Rudolf Hess was present at the Games most days, entertaining foreign dignitaries of the participating nations. A common interest in aviation led him to strike up a casual friendship with the Duke of Hamilton and the seeds were sown to establish an Anglo-German League in London. The Dukes of Hamilton and Kent, Lords Derby, Astor, Dunglass, Bedford and Halifax and Sir Samuel Hoare and David Lloyd George in the House of Commons were all suspected of affiliation to the League in the 1930's.

In the summer of 1913 the nineteen-year-old Edward Prince of Wales had paid a visit to his blood relatives in Germany and made it clear he was pro-German. At the death of King George V on the 20th of February 1936 the Prince of Wales ascended to the throne but, after 325 days as King Edward VIII, he abdicated in favour of marriage to Mrs Wallis-Simpson, a twice-divorced American socialite. As Duke and Duchess of Windsor they settled in Paris and, on the 18th of October 1937, paid a visit to Hitler's Germany. There was an uproar in Britain when it became evident to the public the Windsor's had sailed from Le Havre to Hamburg on a German liner. They were entertained in Berlin by Göering and Göebbels and met with Hitler at his Berghof in Berchtesgaden on October 22nd. Hess led the motorcade which transported the Windsor's from Berlin to the Führer's mountain retreat in Bavaria. At their meeting Adolf Hitler probed the Duke about his relationship with his brother,

King George VI, and his thoughts about regaining the throne of England with his Duchess as his Queen at his side. The Führer was fully aware of the Windsors' sympathetic attitude towards Nazi Germany and hoped that the Duke could regain the British throne from King George VI. Britain might then be ready to unite with the Nazi regime to achieve his lifetime ambition -- the crushing of Soviet Russia and Bolshevism. The Duchess of Windsor enthusiastically favoured the proposal but the Duke had his reservations, especially about Winston Churchill's obstructive attitude to any further upheaval involving the British monarchy.

During 1937 and 1938, and in conjunction with Himmler's SS battalions and the Waffen SS, Rudolf Hess was mainly concerned with setting up fifth column cells in the European countries destined for German occupation in the Führer's programme for 'Lebensraum'. His efforts paid dividends on the 16th of February 1938, with a bloodless 'Anschluss' in Austria and, on October 1st, annexation of the Sudetenland in Czechoslovakia. . As agreed by Prime Ministers Chamberlain of Britain and Edouard Daladier of France, German troops occupied the rest of Czechoslovakia on the 15th of March 1939. In the same month the two Prime Ministers pledged their support for Poland should she be unlawfully attacked by any of her neighbours. On the 1st of September 1939 Germany invaded Poland and, within a fortnight, all Polish resistance had been overcome. Poland capitulated and was partitioned into two sectors, the eastern half occupied by Russia and the western half under control of Nazi Germany. In accordance with their promise to Poland Great Britain declared war on Nazi Germany at 11:00am on Sunday the 3rd of September 1939.

Prime Minister Neville Chamberlain's appeasement policy

in 1938 had failed to prevent an European conflict. Adolf Hitler had been reassured by von Ribbentrop's prediction that Britain and France would not intervene if he struck eastwards into Poland and onwards into Russia. The Allies kept their promise to Poland and declared war on Germany, but not against Soviet Russia who had signed a Non-Aggression Pact with Hitler in August 1939 and subsequently shared the spoils and occupied the eastern half of Poland. The Führer now had to change his plans. He decided to deal with Britain and France first before he could attempt to subjugate the USSR. For six months, during the so-called 'phoney war', the two sides measured up to each other on the Western Front, on the border between neutral Belgium and France.

The German Juggernaut started moving on the 10th of April 1940 with a peaceful occupation of Denmark followed, after three weeks' fighting, by Norway's capitulation. On the 10th of May the German blitzkrieg attacked the Allies, advancing through Belgium and Holland and, within six weeks, 330,000 Allied soldiers were evacuated from Dunkirk. Thereafter French resistance crumbled and their government, under Marshall Pétain, signed an armistice on the 25th of June 1940. Britain now stood alone. After the Norway setback Winston Churchill replaced Neville Chamberlain as Prime Minister and Benito Mussolini took Italy into the conflict on the 12th of June 1940, at the time when a shattered France was on its knees and resisting alone against Hitler's military might.

German Forces were approaching Paris in mid-June 1940 and the Duke and Duchess of Windsor fled south to Biarritz. In early July they were living in a villa outside Madrid and by mid-July German agents reported the Windsor's were in neutral Portugal. Travelling incognito, and with the Führer's permission, Hess arrived at Hotel Albatroz in Cascais, thirty miles outside Lisbon, on the 3rd of August only to find the Duke and Duchess had reluctantly been taken abroad a British destroyer two days previously and whisked away to serve the rest of the war as Governor of the Bahamas. Before he left Portugal the Duke was heard to express an opinion "Heavy bombing raids will induce Britain to sue for peace."

During the two months immediately after the Dunkirk evacuation the Nazis made several futile approaches to the British Government seeking an armistice. By the end of July, Adolf Hitler was exasperated and turned to Reichsmarshall Hermann Göering and his Luftwaffe to gain control of the airspace over the English Channel and allow his Wehrmacht to undertake 'Operation Sealion', a seaborne invasion of Britain. The Battle of Britain in the air commenced in earnest on the 12th of August 1940. Britain's fighter pilots faced Luftwaffe raids by combined German bombers and fighters and both sides suffered heavy losses in aircraft and aircrew. Göering's bombers failed to subdue the gallant Londoners whose will to resist the Nazi blitz was only strengthened by the air raids. Likewise the Luftwaffe failed to master the RAF pilots who henceforth were called 'The Few'. Based on sound evidence, and arguing she posed no immediate threat to Germany, the Führer postponed his plans to invade England on the 12th of October, 1940, despite warnings against waging war on two fronts. Hitler now concentrated on preparations for an all-out attack on the USSR. Code-named Operation Barbarossa the invasion was pencilled-in to start on May 15th, 1941.

Adolf Hitler's start date for Operation Barbarossa was placed in jeopardy by his Axis partner in crime in Italy. Without consulting his co-dictator, Mussolini ordered his armies in

Albania to launch an attack on Greece in November 1940. At first the assault met with success and the Duce's armies advanced into northern Greece but became bogged down in the wintry snow-covered mountains. When fighting re-started in the spring of 1941, Italian forces were driven back into Albania and the Führer was forced to send German troops to bail out Mussolini. Destined for Operation Barbarossa, front-line German infantry were diverted southwards through Yugoslavia and into Greece, which was overrun in three weeks. Allied troops were evacuated to Crete and, in one of the bloodiest campaigns of the war, German paratroopers had captured the island by the end of May 1941. Spread thinly on the ground German armies were involved in fighting in North Africa, Greece and Crete and Hitler had to postpone Barbarossa until the 22nd of June 1941.

Rudolf Hess had made up his mind to fly to Britain to negotiate an armistice as early as October 1940. On returning from his abortive mission to Portugal in an attempt to contact the Duke of Windsor, Hess had lunch with Professor Karl Haushofer to explore the feasibility of flying to Britain to negotiate a peace treaty with the British government. Haushofer assured him that his son, Albrecht, could facilitate a meeting with the Duke of Hamilton and possibly other members of the Anglo-German League but, in the present state of aerial conflict over the English Channel, such a flight would be suicidal and doomed to fail. Stubborn and determined Hess presented his plans before Hitler. His 'stupid' idea was immediately dismissed by Hitler as a crazy fantasy. Needing to please his master in some way Rudolf then offered his services to fly missions with the Luftwaffe. Hitler exploded and banned Hess from flying for a year. Rudolf Hess left the Chancellery mortally offended by the Führer's rebuff and with his tail between his legs. His master's telling-off only strengthened Hess's determination to do something to help the war effort and, as a spin-off, reinstate himself in the Führer's good books. As evidence of his dedication there are intimations that, between April 20th and 23rd 1941, either Hess himself, or his envoy, travelled to Madrid for a secret meeting with Sir Samuel Hoare and British Pro-peace representatives. The discussions, if they ever occurred, arrived at no workable agreement and the Pro-peace delegation returned to London to continue their efforts to secure an armistice between Britain and Germany.

In April 1941 Adolf Hitler was heavily involved with the military implications of his impending major assault on the U.S.S.R. British nightly bombing raids on German cities and industrial centres were taking effect and the Führer began to revisit the logic of not fighting on two fronts. He decided to re-examine the feasibility of striking Britain out of the equation by sending a peace envoy across the Channel for armistice negotiations. The Führer's first choice was Willheim Ernst Böhle, but Böhle was not known in Britain and carried no political clout. Adolf Hitler came to a conclusion that the most suitable candidate might be his Deputy. Hess would carry weight with the British government and could be relied on to sacrifice his life before divulging any secret plans for the future conduct of military operations in Eastern Europe. In his usual fashion the Führer suggested this course of action in a private conversation with Rudolf Hess during the last few days of April 1941. No records, or minutes, were kept of the meeting and Hitler made it abundantly clear to Rudolf that, should this mission fail he, the Führer, would deny any knowledge about Hess's proposed flight. Within a week the Führer had made a complete U-turn. He now granted permission for Hess to fly to meet a British peace delegation but only on neutral ground, preferably in Sweden. Hess had never disobeyed the Führer's orders at any time in their twenty-one years' association but, on this occasion, he took umbrage. His plans to fly to England were foremost in his mind and he was determined to carry out his peace mission come Hell and high water.

THE FLIGHT

10TH MAY 1941

A dolf Hitler's military competence during the French campaign impressed even the most sceptical Wehrmacht generals and, by early 1941, their main anxiety was the wisdom of conducting warfare on two fronts. Rudolf Hess supported this view especially when the Wehrmacht's crack infantry had to be deployed to help out his Axis partner in Greece and Crete and to reinforce Rommel's ground forces in North Africa. At a War Cabinet Council on the 10th of April 1941, Hitler made a decision to postpone Operation Barbarossa from the 15th of May to the 22nd of June. Rudolf Hess was present at the meeting and fully aware of this decision. He again queried the wisdom of fighting on two fronts. The Führer frostily dismissed his concern out of hand, reassuring the War Cabinet he was in full control of the situation, but the seeds of doubt were again sown in the Führer's mind. In April 1941 Britain was in dire straits, constantly bombarded from the air by the Luftwaffe and with her vital supply line across the Atlantic from the USA and Canada in danger of collapsing under intense pressure from Admiral Doenitz's U-boats. Hitler realised a successful peace mission would allow Germany a clear-cut opportunity to attack Russia without the concern of being stabbed in the back. The Führer did not wish to be identified with the proposed flight and, should it fail, he intended to deny any knowledge of it. Should it succeed, however, the Führer would be the first person to congratulate the peace envoy on his diplomatic expertise and his courage in flying solo into the heart of enemy territory.

Under Hess's instruction, tentative approaches to the Duke of Hamilton for a meeting in neutral Lisbon had been made by Albrecht Haushofer as early as the 23rd of September 1940. The letter was intercepted by MI6 and a negative reply was not received in Berlin until a few weeks before Hess flew to Scotland. By March 1941 Hitler had agreed in secret Hess should re-explore his offer to undertake a peace mission either to Britain or, failing this, to a neutral country. Albrecht Haushofer now called on Marcus Wallenberg, a Swedish banker and undercover agent, to arrange a reception party for the emissary's plane at the Duke's estate in Scotland. The date of the plane's arrival in British aerospace was to be relayed, via Sweden, to MI6 in London using a prearranged coded message. The identity of the plane's pilot was not divulged either to the Swedish agent or to MI6. Typically, and within a week, Adolf Hitler had changed his mind once again and forbade Hess to even think about heading for England but he had agreed to a peace mission to a neutral country. Sweden was the obvious choice and Albrecht Haushofer made a second set of arrangements for a meeting in Stockholm between Rudolf Hess and British delegates.

On the 5th of May 1941 Rudolf Hess and the Führer had a two-hour private meeting at the Reichschancellery in Berlin. It is inconceivable to imagine that their secret discussions on this occasion were not entirely about Hess's proposed mission to Sweden. It is equally inconceivable to suggest Adolf Hitler had no prior knowledge of Hess's flight. They must have discussed the flight path over Germany and the arrangements made by Haushofer for Hess's reception in Stockholm. Finally, the

Deputy Führer was ordered to carry a mental note of the peace settlement which Hitler was prepared to offer the British delegates. The missionary plane would be unarmed and Hess was ordered not to carry on his person any firearms, objects of identification and any incriminating documents. Rudolf was instructed to write to the Führer before take-off stressing the flight was his personal decision and, if his mission failed, Hitler could always claim it was undertaken by his Deputy in an unsound state of mind. Hitler thought it was unnecessary to remind Hess not to divulge any Party secrets to the British delegates. The British Government was already aware that Barbarossa had been postponed and was informed by secret agents in Portugal at the end of May that a new date for Germany's assault on the U.S.S.R. would be in late June 1941. At the end of the secret meeting in the Chancellery the two senior Nazis formally shook hands and Hess offered his master an exaggerated Nazi salute. He then turned on his heels and strutted out of the Führer's study. Five days later Hess boarded his plane at Augsburg and flew to Scotland and into captivity in Britain. The two men were never to meet each other again.

Forty-eight hours after Rudolf Hess landed in Scotland Adolf Hitler announced to the German nation, and the world, that his Deputy had defected to Britain in a disturbed mental state and the Nazi Government had no knowledge of his flight beforehand. The Deputy Führer had finally made up his mind to fly to Britain in October 1940. Previously he had never done anything without the Führer's explicit permission but, for once in their twenty-one year association in the Nazi Party, Hess disobeyed his master and left Augsburg with the express intention of making for the Duke of Hamilton's estate in Scotland. Dr Willi Messerschmitt, owner of the Messerschmitt factory in Augsburg, had provided Hess with a fighter plane equipped for a long-distance flight in January 1941 and over the next three months Hess had made over twenty practice runs in the Me110 to familiarize himself with the aircraft. Hitler must have known, via secret agents, that Rudolf Hess was planning a long flight in the foreseeable future and by May 1941 he thought he knew his Deputy's destination. The Führer went berserk when he learnt, on Sunday 11th of May, that contrary to his explicit orders Rudolf Hess, his dependable and loyal Deputy, had flown to Scotland and not to Stockholm.

Saturday the 10th of May 1941 was a gloriously sunny day in Munich and the weather forecast over the North Sea was favourable. In the morning Hess took his four-year-old son, 'Buz,' for a walk along the Isar river and shared a light lunch with Alfred Rosenberg, who left early in the afternoon to journey to join the Führer at Obersalzburg. It is conceivable Rosenberg carried a verbal message to the Führer informing him of his Deputy's intended flight later that day. If he did, Hitler would have concluded Hess's mission was directed towards a meeting with British diplomats in Sweden. After lunch Hess dressed in his light blue Luftwaffe uniform, said his goodbyes to his wife and son and, at 3:30 p.m., he was driven from his house in Munich to the airfield at Augsburg by his adjutant, Lieutenant Karlheinz Pintsch. The ground staff at Hunstteten airfield had been warned to prepare the Deputy Führer's aeroplane for a long-distance flight. Hess's fighter was a series D Messerschmitt B (f) 110 equipped with two spare 900-litre drop tanks and a radio compass. Hess's target in Britain was an airstrip at the Duke of Hamilton's ancestral home at Dungavel, 16 miles south of Glasgow and over 800 miles by direct flight from Augsburg and at the extreme range for his

Messerschmitt fighter. Once Hess reached his destination, if he ever did make it, there would be no returning to his homeland. At Hunstteten's orderly room Hess handed a sealed envelope to his adjutant with strict instructions to wait four hours for the Me110's return to Augsburg. Should his plane not get back by that time, Lieutenant Pintsch was ordered to make his way to the Berghof at Berchtesgaden and to deliver Rudolph's letter by hand to Adolf Hitler in person.

Rudolf Hess was a competent pilot and an expert navigator. His Messerschmitt 110 took off from Augsburg at 5:15p.m. German Summer Time and took a northwesterly course for 380 miles, flying over Bonn and Arnhem to reach the Zuider Zee. He then deviated eastwards for 40 minutes towards Denmark to avoid British long-distance radar and possibly to convince German radar-tracking stations he was on his way to Sweden. After 40 minutes he swung back westwards and climbed to 5,000 feet for his two-hour flight across the North Sea. German radio ground control lost contact with Hess's Messerschmitt when it was fifty miles out over the North Sea. At around 9:45 p.m. he was within range of Northumbrian radar stations and was identified as Raid 42. The Northumbrian coastline was shrouded in sea mist but, though low on the horizon, the sun was still too bright for safety. Rudolf Hess now flew a rectangular course for 40 minutes to await darkness and jettisoned his fuel reserve drop tanks before crossing the English coastline at Bamburgh. An RAF station at Outon was alerted to track and intercept the stray aircraft and, if it resisted, to shoot it down. Two RAF Spitfires were scrambled but, due to the enveloping darkness and the ground mist over the hills, they failed to identify the plane. After climbing to 6,000 feet over the Cheviots, Hess flew his Me110 at 300mph, and at a low level, across the Scottish border in a north-westerly direction. His progress was tracked across Scotland by members of the Royal Observer Corps. Two Hurricanes of 245 Squadron, based at Aldergrove in Northern Ireland, were scrambled to intercept the Me110. A confusion of orders forced the Czech pilots to return to base. The low-flying German aircraft proceeded westwards in the gathering gloom in an attempt to reach the airstrip at Dungavel. Speculation at the time was rife that the British Secret Service had arranged for a runway to be lit up to assist the Me110 to land on terra firma but the landing lights were never displayed.

Hess's Messerschmitt missed its intended landmark and, at 10:50 p.m., it flew out over the West Coast of Scotland into the North Channel, connecting the Irish Sea with the Atlantic Ocean. With near-empty fuel tanks, and losing height rapidly, Hess turned his aircraft back towards the mainland and his intended landing site at Dungavel. He was now flying at a perilously low level and Rudolf had no option but to bail out. Climbing rapidly to 6,000 feet he turned his engine off and attempted a half-loop. The increase in G-force caused him to pass out and when he came to his aircraft was flying upside down and on the point of stalling. He pushed himself backwards out of the open cockpit and parachuted towards earth. The Deputy Führer hit the ground with force and chipped a bone in his right ankle.

Forty-seven-year-old Rudolf Hess had miraculously arrived at Eaglesham in Renfrewshire in one piece having dropped onto a meadow 12 miles west of Dungavel House and 200 yards away from a farmhouse. His plane crashed to earth two thousand yards to the north of the farmyard.. The flight from Augsburg had taken a few minutes short of five hours at an average cruising speed of 220m.p.h and was shining testimony to Rudolf Hess's misguided bravery and navigational skills. He landed at around 11:10pm, the official lighting-up time in Scotland in May 1941. The first 'Englander' to come face to face with the Deputy Führer was a stocky man in shirtsleeves, wielding a pitchfork, and shouting in a strange, incomprehensible Glaswegian accent.

Back at Hunstteten airfield in Augsburg, Lieutenant Karlheinz Pintsch waited the prearranged four hours for Hess's return and, at around 9:15pm, he telephoned the Telecommunications Centre in Berlin to ascertain weather conditions over Scotland and to ensure radio-direction signals were being received from the errant Messerschmitt. This started alarm bells ringing and Hermann Göering was urgently contacted. Without consulting the Führer he, in turn, ordered Adolf Galland's Fighter Group in North Germany to take to the air and shoot down Hess's Messerschmitt adding, "The Deputy Führer has gone mad and is deserting to England." Galland sent up two Messerschmitts from each of his three squadrons but it was a futile exercise. Darkness was descending and Hess's Me110 was well out over the North Sea when Galland's six aircraft took to the air. Galland was forced to report back to Göering the sortie had failed. This incident is an important indication that Reichsmarshall Göering had prior knowledge that Hess was planning a mercy flight, not specifically to England, but probably to Stockholm in Sweden.

Karlheinz Pintsch travelled overnight by train to the Berghof at Berchtesgaden and, on Sunday morning 11th of May 1941, he presented Rudolf Hess's bombshell letter to the Führer. Adolf Hitler flew into a towering rage and the unfortunate Pintsch was rewarded for his trouble by being immediately arrested and incarcerated for twenty months. Albrecht Haushofer was also imprisoned but was released after a fortnight in gaol. On the night of the 12th of May, Joseph Göebbels, the Nazi Party Propaganda Minister announced to the World that, in an unsound frame of mind, Rudolf Hess had flown to Britain without the Führer's consent and prior knowledge.

THE FIRST ELEVEN DAYS
IN CAPTIVITY

10th – 21st MAY 1941

Double British Summer Time was instituted by the government at the beginning of the war to allow maximum daylight hours for Scottish farmers to harvest their crops. David Mclean, a 45-year-old bachelor, was employed as a ploughman at Floors' dairy farm in Eaglesham in Renfrewshire, five miles west of Paisley and sixteen miles south of Glasgow. On the 10th of May 1941, Mclean was in his cottage preparing for bed at around 10:30 pm. Petrol for his ancient tractor was rationed and he had been toiling hard all day ploughing a field with a shire horse and taking advantage of the lengthy daylight hours. The sun had set and twilight was gradually fading into darkness. On the radio London was again suffering one of its heaviest air raids since the Blitz began. Mclean walked his shepherd dogs outside in the farmyard to stretch his legs before retiring for the night. While he was standing by the barn at around 10:40pm, he heard an aircraft approaching rapidly from the east and, within seconds, an aeroplane flew at low-level over Paisley heading westwards. Mclean could not see the plane but he was conscious of a large flying object hurtling through the air. He lit a pipe and 20 minutes later a plane was again approaching, this time from the southwest, and hurtling directly over his cottage. The deafening crescendo overhead came to an abrupt halt within a few seconds and the plane crashed to the ground about two miles away to the north. David Mclean peered northwards across his fields in the direction of the aircraft's flight path and had an impression of something white floating to earth about two hundred yards away from where he was standing. Grabbing a pitchfork from the barn he ran into the meadow to investigate.

Rudolf Hess's risky parachute descent from his Messerschmitt resulted in a heavy landing, cracking a bone in his right ankle. By the time Mclean got to him he was sitting up on the ground, slightly stunned and attempting to unravel himself from the parachute shrouds and harness. The man on the ground wore a leather airman's jacket and flying boots but, in the dim light, the farmer was unable to ascertain his nationality. Wielding his pitchfork menacingly Mclean asked, "Are ye a Nazi enemy or are ye one o' ours?" "Not Nazi. British friend," the leather-jacketed pilot replied. Mclean assisted him to hobble to the farmhouse kitchen and his mother came downstairs and brewed a pot of tea. Once he had settled down the parachutist announced his name was Hauptman Alfred Horn and he had flown from Germany to meet the Duke of Hamilton. Within half an hour a Home Guard Officer and two Gunners appeared on the scene and 'Alfred Horn' kept repeating a request for them to make contact with the Duke of Hamilton at Dungavel where a reception committee awaited his arrival at a local airstrip. The Home Guard Officer took the foreign pilot to Busby Police Station and he was quickly transferred in a military vehicle to the Medical Centre at Maryhill Army Barracks on the outskirts of Glasgow. Here he was kept under guard while his ankle was strapped and he spent his first night on British soil at the Medical Centre. In the morning he had changed his story. 'Alfred Horn' now claimed he was Rudolf Hess, the Deputy Führer, and he had come across to Britain to save humanity. He added he was expected at Dungavel by the Duke of Hamilton and members of the Anglo-German League. They would arrange a meeting with British negotiators and maybe with King George VI. It is of interest to note that, in the early hours of Sunday the 11th of May, the Duke of Kent and the Duke of Buccleach were involved in a minor traffic accident whilst driving on a country lane near Dungavel House. It may be pure conjecture to insinuate they might have been expecting to meet a German peace envoy at Dungavel but it fuels speculation the Pro-peace Party knew that a Nazi envoy was flying to Scotland on the 10th of May 1941.

Serving as a Wing Commander in the Royal Air Force, and stationed at Turnhouse outside Edinburgh, the Duke of Hamilton was the first British official to see Hess. It was at 11:00am on the next day. The Nazi pilot requested him to alert members of the Pro-peace group and to ask King George VI for his parole to allow him to outline Hitler's peace proposals to the British Government, but not to Winston Churchill. He also asked if the Duke could let his family know that he was alive and had landed safely in England. That same night the Duke flew south to London and reported directly to Winston Churchill, spending the weekend at Ditchley Park in Oxfordshire. The meeting took place at 3:00am on the 12th of May and Churchill demanded positive proof of identity of the renegade Nazi pilot. He ordered the Duke to return to Glasgow on the same day accompanied by Ivone Kirkpatrick, an MI6 secret agent and a councillor at the British Embassy in Berlin in the 1930's. The man in bed at Maryhill Barracks had no identification papers, merely two photographs of himself as a child, Professor Karl Haushofer's visiting card, a Leica camera belonging to Frau Hess, ten Reichsmark banknotes, a torch and twenty-eight small tins of homeopathic remedies. The Duke had never been in close contact with the Deputy Führer but Kirkpatrick had met Hess at diplomatic functions in the 1930s and was able to make an unequivocal identification. The Duke and the MI6 agent returned to London to report directly to the Prime Minister. Winston Churchill now demanded information from the high-ranking Nazi officer. By the time the Duke of Hamilton and Ivone Kirkpatrick returned north to Scotland on the following day Rudolf Hess has been moved and was now under guard at Buchanan Castle where a three-hour interview took place after midnight 13th May. Still on a 'high', and elated by his successful flight, Hess's attitude throughout was that of a superior, munificent enemy offering a reprieve to an otherwise doomed and defeated country. He monopolized the meeting with a lengthy tirade outlining Germany's objectives in demanding a negotiated peace and stressed he did not wish to discuss terms with Prime Minister Churchill. Details of the peace terms were only briefly touched upon. Hess was consistent in one respect - he refused to divulge any information about Hitler's plans for invading Russia and of Germany's military and economic capabilities. All the while Hess assumed he was dealing with Pro-peace members and it suited Kirkpatrick's purpose that Hess had no intimation he was a senior executive at MI6. Kirkpatrick made a full report at the Cabinet War Rooms in Whitehall on 14th May and Winston Churchill flatly refused to see Hess or to consider Adolf Hitler's 'peace proposals.' He agreed, however, to go along with MI6's plans of allowing Hess to believe the British Government were in ardent discussion about them.

During the dark days of 1941, when Britain stood alone against the might of Nazi Germany, Winston Churchill was acutely aware that some gentry, and politicians, were only too ready to accept defeat and to sue for an armistice. The Pro-peace group was active in Parliament. As recently as May 7th the Prime Minister had survived a vote of 'no confidence' in the House of Commons, instigated by Lloyd George and Sir Samuel Hoare, and strongly supported by the Pro-peace Duke of Bedford in the House of Lords. The mounting pressure on Churchill to negotiate an armistice was probably an orchestrated campaign in Parliament to coincide with Hess's peace mission, strongly suggesting some members in the Government, and a few aristocratic Pro-peace activists, were fully aware a Nazi envoy was expected to arrive in Britain, specifically in Scotland, on May10th. For global consumption, Winston Churchill went along with the Nazi pronouncement on 12th May that 'the Deputy Führer had flown to Britain in a confused state of mind'. The British and German statements varied in only one respect -- Churchill asserted Hess had defected to Britain to escape from the Gestapo, but the Germans stressed Hess had undertaken his flight in a confused mental state, without the Führer's knowledge and consent.

During the two World Wars of the 20th Century the Tower of London was used for incarcerating aliens accused of treason, or espionage, and, if found guilty, for immediate execution. Winston Churchill had decided on day one to treat Hess as a prisoner-of-war, but wanted to frighten the Deputy Führer and ordered he should be taken to the Tower for a few days and intensely interrogated. The transfer occurred overnight on Friday 16th May by express train from Glasgow to London. The Nazi prisoner remained in the Tower for only five counterproductive days. The Tower guards were instructed to mention *Herren* Waldberg and Meier within Hess's hearing.

These two Germans were Nazi spies imprisoned in the Tower and subsequently hanged on 11th December 1940, a fact of which Rudolf Hess was made fully aware. Major Frank Foley, head of German Section A at MI6 and a secret operative at the British Embassy in Berlin in the 1930s, was nominated to interrogate Hess and to answer back directly to the Prime Minister. Any information gleaned from the prisoner was only to be released to the public on Winston Churchill's say-so. Rudolf Hess soon came to realise that his interrogators were only interested in Hitler's intentions and plans towards Russia. The garrulous Nazi who arrived in Scotland now became a sullen, introspective hulk, like a spoilt child unable to get his own way. He was also acutely conscious he might suffer the same fate as Meier and Waldberg, and all his efforts to broker a peace between Germany and Britain would have been in vain. Hess withdrew into his shell and shut up like a clam. The interrogators gave up and realised they were getting nowhere. Winston Churchill became disillusioned by the military knowledge exhibited by the high-ranking Nazi in the Tower and sanctioned his removal to a detention centre for further interrogation. Now code-named 'Jonathan', Rudolf Hess was transferred to Mytchett Place, Aldershot, on Wednesday 21 May 1941.

In May 1941, Soviet Russia was tied to a Non-aggression Pact with Nazi Germany. Joseph Stalin was convinced at the time the British Secret Service knew beforehand about Hess's flight and even suggested the Deputy Führer had been invited to fly across the English Channel. At a meeting in the Kremlin in December 1943, Stalin challenged Churchill and disbelieved the P.M.'s denial that a secret plot was in place in 1941. Churchill was offended by Uncle Joe's insinuation. With a sly grin Stalin pointed out that many things happened, even in Russia, which were not reported to him by the Soviet Secret Service. This was also almost certainly true in Britain during the 1939-45 war.

MYTCHETT PLACE: CAMP 'Z'

21st MAY 1941- 22nd JULY 1942

Once the identity of the Nazi pilot, purporting to be Rudolf Hess, had been established the War Cabinet in Whitehall decided he should be treated as a privileged prisoner-of-war. Churchill himself insisted he should be kept under lock and key, guarded by his Majesty's Footguards, denied newspapers and the radio bulletins and any communication with the outside world. The carefully chosen site for the Nazi prisoner was a mansion three miles north of Aldershot in Surrey. Mytchett Place, or 'Camp Z', had the advantage of being completely secluded with installed bugging devices in every room. Intended for up to five senior war captives Rudolf Hess became sole prisoner occupant of Camp Z on the 21st of May 1941.

Captain James Sutherland, a temporary Company Commander with the 2nd Battalion Scots Guards, was selected for duty at Camp Z and was ordered to attend a briefing at MI6 Headquarters in Whitehall, London on Saturday the 17th of May 1941. The twenty-three year old Guard's officer was a native of Tayside in Scotland. His father, Brigadier Hamish Sutherland, had been awarded an M.C. at the Somme battlefield in1916 when serving with the Scots Guards and it was predestined James would follow in his father's footsteps. Tall, blonde and blue-eyed, James studied Germanic languages at Cambridge University and graduated MA in April 1937. He then attended Sandhurst and was commissioned into the Scots Guards in

March 1938. In 1941 his regiment was stationed at Pirbright only three miles distant as the crow flies from Mytchett Place.

In a basement-cum-interrogation room at MI6, three men were seated behind a desk when James Sutherland reported mid-morning on the 17th of May. Dressed in a grey pinstripe suit, and sporting a red carnation, the head of MI6, Sir Stewart Menzies, introduced the uniformed officers sitting with him. "On my right, Major Frank Foley, and on my left, Lieutenant Colonel Malcolm Scott, Commandant of Camp Z." Scanning a sheaf of notes on his desk the Chairman opened the meeting.

"Captain Sutherland! We have a highly sensitive task for your Scots Guards. A high-ranking Nazi, whom we shall refer to as 'Jonathan', has landed in our lap. He is at present at the Tower of London and will shortly be transferred to Camp Z, a secure house in Surrey, for further debriefing. Your Battalion is required to mount guard on Camp Z until further notice. Under no circumstances are you, or your officers and guardsmen, to reveal the identity of the prisoner. 'Jonathan' must be kept under wraps at all times. Is that clear, Sutherland?"

"Yes Sir," James replied. Sir Stewart Menzies then turned towards the Lieutenant Colonel sitting at his left hand.

"Colonel Scott, will you fill in with details of the guard duties?"

The uniformed Camp Commandant Colonel outlined James's duties.

"At Camp Z you will provide a detachment of twenty-four guardsmen and a senior NCO for protecting the compound perimeter, You will also be in charge of a dozen junior officers and subalterns who will mount a 24-hour guard on 'Jonathan' in his detention quarters inside the House. I am in charge of seeing that Camp Z complex runs smoothly. You will concentrate on making sure 'Jonathan' does not escape and, of equal importance, that no one from the outside can get at the prisoner. Report to me at Mytchett Place tomorrow at 1030 hours and we'll run though the drill."

The Chairman shuffled his papers and readdressed James.

"That's it in a nutshell. Any questions, Captain Sutherland?"

"No, Sir," James replied and prepared to leave when Major Foley spoke up for the first time.

"I see from your Curriculum Vitae you majored in Germanic languages at Cambridge. I suggest you do not divulge your knowledge of German to 'Jonathan'. If you learn anything from him that might be useful for us to know you must pass on the information immediately. You will meet with 'Jonathan' in the next few days." The Chairman's face broke into a friendly smile. He nodded his head and James was dismissed. The Scots Guards captain rose to his feet, saluted, turned sharply on his heels and marched out of the interrogation room. The Committee looked at each other and smiled. The Chairman wound up the proceedings.

"That officer is the right man for the job."

On Sunday morning the 18th of May, as ordered, Captain James Sutherland met Lieutenant Colonel Scott at Camp Z, at 1030 hours. Mytchett Place is an 1880 extension and conversion of a derelict farmhouse first built in 1779. Situated at the edge of a woodland, and only approachable down a 200-yard driveway, it has four reception rooms and a large kitchen on the ground floor and eight bedrooms and two bathrooms upstairs. The quarters set apart for 'Jonathan' were at the top of a flight of stairs leading up to the first floor. The entrance to the prisoner's suite was protected by an L-shaped metal grille, a sentry point for a guard stationed outside the corridor leading to a small bedroom and a larger sitting room containing a sofa, two armchairs and a writing desk. The Camp Commandant explained that two junior officers would be on duty for each 24 hours, one in the grille cage alternating with a second on call in a bedroom adjacent to the prisoner's suite. Other bedrooms were occupied by Lt Col. Gibson Graham, a duty M.O., Major H.V.Dicks and two Intelligence Corps Officers and, on the ground floor a suite had been allocated for James, the Guard Commander. Outside the southern aspect of the mansion there was a lawn and an exercise yard and the entire compound was surrounded by two cordons of barbed wire fencing with spotlights and alarm bells positioned at intervals along the perimeter. Guardsmen and junior officers off duty at Camp Z were accommodated in the Army School of Hygiene about two miles down the road at Mytchett. In time Mytchett villagers Christened the prisoner at Camp Z, "The Squire of Mychett Green."

Captain James Sutherland had barely 48 hours to settle in at Camp Z before an order came to pick up 'Jonathan' at the Tower of London. The transference was arranged for the afternoon of Wednesday the 21st of May to avoid nightly German bombing raids on London. Even before he left for the Tower with an armed Scots Guards escort, James had strong convictions that 'Jonathan' would turn out to be Rudolf Hess. His flight to Britain had already been announced on the radio and Prime Minister Churchill's resounding speech in the House of Commons, defeating a vote of no confidence, were the two major discussion topics for discussion for Britain's wartime citizens. The military convoy was made up of three vehicles. Captain Sutherland and three armed Scots guardsmen travelled in one car and a Coldstream Guards Colonel and three of his guardsmen in the other. The third vehicle was a windowless army ambulance. Lieutenant Colonel Gibson Graham, an RAMC doctor who had accompanied Hess from Buchanan Castle in Scotland and now had the dubious pleasure of escorting him in the back of the ambulance to his destination at Camp Z. The convoy left Tower Wharf at 3:40 p.m. and arrived at Mytchett place at around 5:30pm.

At Camp Z Rudolf Hess was escorted upstairs to his quarters and, despite the fact it was early evening, he climbed into bed in his pyjamas. He was introduced to the personnel who would be looking after him, Captain Sutherland, Major Foley and an MI6 colleague and Lieutenant Colonel Scott, Camp Z's Commandant. Believing his first two contacts in Scotland were his main channel for arranging a meeting with the Pro-peace group and King George VI, Hess asked if he could see the Duke of Hamilton and Ivone Kirkpatrick again. Reassured by Major Foley his request would be passed on to the British authorities, Hess settled down for the night.

Frank Foley and two MI6 interrogators had been deputized to supervise Hess's debriefing and Foley was well qualified to do so. Between 1923 and the outbreak of World War II he was stationed at the British Embassy in Berlin. Ostensibly a Passport Control Officer he was, in reality, head of the Secret Intelligence Service in Berlin. Ivone Kirkpatrick had served at the same Consulate in the late 1930's. Fluent in German and French, Foley had attended diplomatic functions and receptions where the Deputy Führer was also present. MI6's ace Intelligence Officer made 'Jonathan's' debriefing his prime occupation during the latter half of 1941 and the spring of 1942. He encouraged James Sutherland to keep close to Rudolf Hess in the knowledge that any information he extracted from the prisoner would be reported directly back to MI6.

The Nazi prisoner James collected at the Tower of London behaved differently to the pilot who had landed eleven days previously on farmer Mclean's meadow in Renfrewshire. Whereas the uninvited Nazi aviator had been excited, loquacious and perfectly sane in Scotland, he had quickly become disillusioned by the lack of respect shown to him. British officials' promises, and their disinclination to meet with him to discuss Hitler's carefully prepared peace proposals, rankled with the Deputy Führer and he felt it was an affront to his high-ranking position within the Nazi Party. He feared his gallant flight as a peace emissary had been in vain and he had failed his idol and mentor, Adolf Hitler. Hess withdrew into his shell and began behaving oddly with prolonged periods of silence and staring vacantly into space, sighing and grunting from time to time. The resident Medical Officer, Lieutenant Colonel Gibson Graham, first reported this peculiar behaviour and suggested 'Jonathan' needed an urgent psychiatric assessment. Brigadier J.R. Rees was called in and he, in turn, appointed Major Henry V. Dicks to replace Dr Graham as Camp Z's resident M.O. Major Dicks took up office on the 1st of June 1944. A Jewish refugee from Estonia, Dicks's appointment was not a qualified success. Hess soon became aware of his Semitic background and the psychiatrist's attitude towards the prisoner was one of the causes for disharmony between the two. Rudolf Hess and Major Dicks never hit it off at Camp Z. Hess trusted Lieutenant Colonel Graham and with his departure 'Jonathan' began exhibiting signs of paranoia, convinced his food was poisoned with drugs and affecting his mental stability. Rudolf took his evening meals with Mess members at Camp Z. He frequently refused food, or asked a fellow officer to swap plates, before he took a bite and, in a perverse way, he connected his paranoia to the arrival of Major Henry V. Dicks at Camp Z.

Captain James Sutherland treated Rudolf Hess with the same courtesy he would accord a senior military officer of any nation. He addressed the prisoner as "Sir," or "*Reichsminister*", at all times and saluted Hess each morning and before he retired to bed at night. James's daily routine at Mytchett place involved mounting a perimeter guard at 0800 hours and inspection of the prisoners' quarters at 0830 hours every day of the week. When the prisoner so desired, James, and an armed guardsman, would accompany 'Jonathan' to the exercise yard at 1100 hours and again for one hour in late afternoon, or evening. During the exercise period Hess strode out rapidly with a strutting, goose-stepping gait and James and the guardsman had their work cut out to keep pace with the Deputy Führer. Hess was impressed with the Scots Guards Captain's politeness and correct attitude towards him and James's Aryan blonde hair and blue eyes were, in all probability, contributory factors in swaying Hess to believe James was his only dependable ally at Mytchett Place. Rudolf Hess was nobody's fool and suspected on day one that his cell was bugged and that Foley and his cronies were Intelligence Officers. Accordingly, whenever he felt in a talkative mood, Hess chose to limit conversation to the exercise period. He did not realise, however, their conversation was religiously reported back verbatim to Major Frank Foley.

Rudolf Hess was prone to violent mood swings and the first few exercise breaks with James Sutherland were conducted with hardly a word spoken. One fine sunny day towards the end of May Rudolf Hess broke silence.

"Captain! Am I eating my food off the same dishes as King George?"

"Why do you say that, Sir?" James Sutherland asked.

"The cup and plates show a crown."

James nearly burst out laughing but controlled himself. The crown was a symbol of ownership by the War Department as indicated by the initials W.D. on the cutlery and crockery. James did not wish to deflate and disillusion Hess and he nodded.

"Yes, *Herr Reichsminister*, you are indeed a highly respected guest of His Majesty."

Rudolf Hess smiled ruefully and recommenced striding around the compound at a rapid pace. Whether he was bluffing, or truly believed he was sharing crockery and utensils used by Royalty, remains questionable.

The exercise walks in the compound with James became a regular feature in Rudolf Hess's daily routine. One morning at the end of May he stopped dead in his tracks and rather un-usually, he stared at James with a mischievous smirk on his face

"In the Mess last night there was a Guards officer with five buttons on the sleeve of his service tunic. He was a Captain, and you are a Captain, but you only have three buttons on each sleeve. Why is that?"

James was impressed with 'Jonathan's' powers of observation and replied:

"He is a Captain in the Welsh Guards. There are five regiments in the King's Household Division, each distinguished by the number of buttons on their uniforms. The Senior Regiment are the Grenadier Guards followed by the Coldstreams, my own Scots, the Irish Guards and, finally, the Welsh Guards who exhibit five buttons on the sleeves of their khaki drill. In peacetime there are, in all, over six thousand guardsmen in the King's household Division and a further four hundred in the Household Cavalry."

Rudolf Hess's face broke into a lopsided grin.

"Does it take over six thousand men to guard your King George? In Germany *mein* Führer has only one S.S. Regiment of one thousand *soldats*."

Pleased with himself at scoring a point over the Scots Guards' officer Hess appeared to be flattered to recognise he was eating off the same crockery as Royalty and guarded by soldiers of King George VI's private footguards. His elation was short-lived and, within half an hour, he was back to his sulky self again.

Captain James Sutherland reported a significant change in Hess's mental outlook on the 31st of May 1941. He was escorting the dejected prisoner on his morning constitutional in the exercise compound when three Spitfires from a nearby fighter station swept overhead in a perfect V formation. Like a child witnessing a new plaything, Hess's blank face was suddenly wreathed in smiles as he shouted *"Achtung* Spitfire." He laughed at his own joke and, for the next five minutes, he related his own recent experiences on his hazardous flight from Augsburg to Scotland. He behaved like an awestruck youth reliving his emotions during the flight but when he came towards the end of his monologue, and described his feelings about the success of his daring enterprise, his face was set in a fixed grimace. He spat out the futility of his actions and the shame he felt his attempt as a peacemaker might end in disaster. Should that happen, Rudolf argued, he would be unable to face his Führer and his Party again and the only solution would be to end it all. Taken aback by Hess's confession James Sutherland wasted no time in reporting to Major Foley and Major Henry V Dicks, the Camp psychiatrist. These two officers were fully aware of Hess's depressive episodes but did not consider him a suicide risk. By this time they knew the Government's Lord Chancellor, Lord Simon, would be seeing Hess in the near future and they felt certain his visit would help to put to rest the prisoner's suicidal fantasies. In the meantime they ordered increased vigilance from the internal guards and the ancillary staff at Mytchett Place.

An event which triggered one of Rudolf Hess's severest depressions occurred on Tuesday the 27th of May 1941. The German battleship, *Bismark*, was sunk by the Royal Navy and the Fleet Air Arm, with the loss of 2,000 men. Hess was deliberately told of the naval disaster by Major Frank Foley on the 28th of May. At first 'Jonathan' did not believe Foley, claiming the Bismark was unsinkable but, by the 30th, the truth had sunk in. Hess slipped into a deep depression, mourning the loss of 2,000 *Kreigsmarine* and blaming the catastrophe on his own failure to stop Britain fighting. For Hess this loss was intolerable and the sinking of the *Bismark* helped to affirm his decision to take his own life. Attempts to wheedle information from 'Jonathan' had met with no success and Hess insisted he would only enter into discussion with a senior member of the British Government, but not Winston Churchill. At the end of the abortive interviews Frank Foley acted as an honest broker and reassured Rudolf Hess that the War Cabinet were continually discussing Adolf Hitler's peace proposals at their daily meetings, a fact which was blatantly untrue, and 'Jonathan' did not believe him.

Hess's repeated requests for an audience with one of Churchill's War Cabinet eventually bore fruit on the 9th of June 1941, but with disastrous consequences. Deliberately, or otherwise, Winston Churchill sent a Jewish Lord Chancellor to interview Hess at Mytchett Place. Lord Simon had an acute legal brain and was an expert in cross-examination but, as a personality, he was frigid and unbending and completely lacking in warmth and charm. These latter requirements were essential in dealing with Hess's inflated ego at this stage of his incarceration. Lord Simon was accompanied by MI6's Ivone Kirkpatrick. Hess outlined Adolf Hitler's peace proposals to the legal tyro who kept interrupting the Deputy Führer demanding to know the consequences for Britain of Europe becoming a German sphere of influence. This attitude, and Lord Simon's antipathy towards the Nazi regime, annoyed the Deputy Führer who burst into a tirade of threats against the British Government. Uncharacteristically Lord Simon retaliated and, in his high-pitched, prissy voice suggested to Hess the British people were not fond of threats and Hitler's proposals would find little favour with the War Cabinet. When Ivone Kirkpatrick and Lord Simon left Camp Z, Hess was in the depths of despair and his hopes of international glory, and restoration into Hitler's favour, crashed about him. Regarding himself as a complete failure he became determined to commit suicide.

James Sutherland became acutely aware of a dramatic change in Hess's behaviour during the days immediately following his meeting with Lord Simon. 'Jonathan' declined to accompany him to the exercise compound, stayed brooding in his quarters and refused to join the officers in the Mess at mealtimes. His paranoia became more pronounced and he was convinced the Jews were poisoning his food and deliberately disturbing his sleep by making loud noises at night. He ate sparsely and kept slivers of bread, cheese and meat in his locker for future chemical analysis as evidence he was being poisoned. His sole confidant at Camp Z was James. In a bout of self-recrimination on June 12th, he confided in James he could no longer trust the British Government and had to admit his glorious attempts as a peace envoy had failed. Finally he confessed he was at the end of his tether and might take steps to end it all. James Sutherland raised the alarm and promptly reported his encounter with Hess to Major Foley. Major Dicks commented that this sort of behaviour was a typical response to adversity in a psychopathic patient. Immediate action was taken to increase vigilance by the guards and medical orderlies at Camp Z.

Six days after Lord Simon's visit Rudolf Hess's attempted suicide ended in failure. At 4:00 am on the 15th of June Hess called the guard outside his bedroom and demanded to see Major Dicks, complaining he was in pain and unable to sleep. He then quickly dressed in his blue-grey Luftwaffe uniform and flying boots and hid in a corner of his darkened bedroom. When he heard the guard unlocking the door in the wire-mesh cage to allow entry for the doctor, Hess rushed through on to the first floor landing, brushing past the guard on duty and hurled himself, feet first, over the banister. He crash-landed in a heap on the tiled floor of the entrance hall, 20 feet below. That the Deputy Führer meant to commit suicide was confirmed by two letters he left in his study, one addressed to Adolf Hitler apologising for his failure to broker a peace settlement with England and the other to his wife, Ilse, hinting that he intended to 'end it all'.

Hess's botched suicide attempt resulted in a fracture to his left femur in two places. Pandemonium broke out at Camp Z. Officers, orderlies and guards appeared from every quarter and gathered around the stricken Deputy Führer. Colonel Scott's orders were countermanded by Major Dicks who refused permission to move Hess and possibly cause further damage.

He also declined to administer morphine for fear of concealing internal injuries. Major Murray, a RAMC orthopaedic specialist, arrived shortly after 5:00am and took charge of the surgical emergency. He administered a hefty dose of morphine, splinted Hess's left leg and supervised his manual transfer back upstairs to his quarters. A decision was made at that time to continue treating Hess in his quarters at Camp Z. A portable X-Ray confirmed a fractured left femur. Major Murray operated on Hess at 10:00pm under pentothal anaesthesia on June 15th. A Steinmann pin was inserted into Hess's left tibia and the leg placed on traction on a Balkan beam apparatus.

Before his anaesthetic Hess had complained of a full bladder and Major Dicks refused to catheterize him. On recovering consciousness Hess was again in agony from his urinary retention and complaining bitterly about pain from his over-distended bladder. Major Dicks was forced to attempt catheterization. During his medical and psychiatric training in Estonia Dicks had acquired little, or no, expertise in urology and his ham-fisted attempts at passing a catheter into Hess's full bladder only produced bellows of pain from the unfortunate patient. Dicks abandoned the surgical assault and 'Jonathan' managed to pass urine naturally later in the morning. After ten weeks in traction Rudolf Hess began mobilization in his room but it was not until early December he was able to come downstairs to the Mess at mealtimes.

During the long weeks of treatment and rehabilitation Hess was visited daily by Major Foley, or one of his MI6 agents, and by Major Dicks and Captain James Sutherland. James sat with Hess for 15 to 20 minutes every day and made a point of being punctual and sympathetic towards the Nazi prisoner. Most of the visits were conducted in stony silence under the wounded

Nazi's penetrating gaze. At other times Hess closed his eyes and pretended to be asleep. James conducted himself in a strict military manner which flattered Hess and allowed him to trust the Guard's Captain. During lucid intervals in his post-traumatic depression he confided in James that his attempt at suicide was due to the Cabinet's failure to allow him to make contact with the Pro-peace Group whom he was sure existed among the aristocracy and gentry in Britain. He wrote two letters from his sick-bed to King George VI – one begging him to use his influence to fix a meeting with the Pro-peace officers and the other to arrange for his repatriation to Germany on health grounds. Neither of these letters were delivered to the King. These two requests were a recurrent theme during his incarceration on British soil during World War II.

On June 23rd Major Frank Foley informed Hess that Germany's attack on Russia had commenced on the previous day in the hope this news would startle the Deputy Führer. On the contrary, Hess gave a fleeting grimace and merely commented:

"At last they have started."

Three days later 'Jonathan' confided in James. "I was expecting Barbarossa to start in May. We had trouble in Greece and the Führer had to postpone the attack. Our glorious armies are now on the way and the war will soon be over. It is imperative for your Government to settle with us to avoid unnecessary bloodshed in Britain after we defeat Russia. I am empowered by *Mein Führer* to negotiate an armistice with Britain. Churchill's Government will not listen. Will you ask your Guard's commander to seek a peaceful solution?"

"I will do that," James replied but he did not respond to 'Jonathan's' request.

The following day Major Dicks bluntly told Hess that his beloved Führer had ordered immediate execution if his ex-Deputy ever set foot in Nazi-occupied Europe. 'Jonathan' reacted violently and shouted at Dicks.

"Lies! Lies! I do not believe you. *Mein Führer* would never allow that to happen." Worried it might be true Hess sank into an abyss of despair and depression which lasted for two weeks. He ate very little food and refused to see, or speak to Major Dicks. During his recovery he restarted conversing with James and he was full of complaints.

"The Camp doctor," referring to Major Dicks, "tried to kill me after my accident. Last week he was short-tempered and I no longer trust him to take care of my health. The Camp Commandant," referring to Lieutenant Colonel Scott, "does not pass on my requests and Major Foley is a British secret agent. I am getting nowhere with these officers. Are you able to help me get repatriated to Germany, *Herr* Captain?"

Astounded by these allegations James decided to lie.

"*Herr Reichsminister!* I am able to pass on your complaints to my Regimental Colonel. Colonel Bruce Wallis will act independently of the officers in this Camp and he has powerful connections in Whitehall and with the Government."

Hess perked up and thanked James, not realising he passed on details of their conversation to Major Foley. James did, however, point out to Major Foley that Jonathan had developed a strong dislike and mistrust towards Major Dicks and suggested a non-Jewish replacement might be productive in stimulating

co-operation from Rudolf Hess. No action was taken to replace Major Dicks during 'Jonathan's' imprisonment at Mytchett Place.

After his abortive suicide attempt there was now serious concern about Hess's sanity. Brigadier J.R. Rees, the War Officer's senior psychiatrist, had been given overall responsibility for his mental health and Major Dicks continued to serve as his medical officer at Camp Z. During Hess's recovery period from his surgical catastrophe Dicks became disenchanted by 'Jonathan's' behaviour. He treated the Deputy Führer with some disdain and 'Jonathan' reciprocated by refusing to cooperate in his psychotherapeutic treatments. Major Dicks diagnosed paranoia, depression and possible overt schizophrenia and advised heavy doses of medication. Hess steadfastly refused to take any tablets, sometimes claiming they were prescribed by Jews with the set intention of poisoning his mind. 'Jonathan's' anti-Semitic fantasies came prominently to the forefront at Mytchett Place and continued throughout his years of captivity in Britain. He openly accused European Jewry and the Bolsheviks for instigating the First and Second World Wars. Despite their doctor-patient incompatibility Major Henry V. Dicks remained Hess's personal psychiatrist at Camp Z until July 1942.

Under instruction by Major Foley, James Sutherland imparted some good news to 'Jonathan' on the 1st of September 1941. James informed Hess that his Regimental Colonel had arranged a visit to Camp Z by Lord Beaverbrook. Born in Canada, William Maxwell Aitken Beaverbrook became a Press Baron, financier and politician in Britain in the 1930s and served as Minister of Supply and Aircraft Production in Churchill's wartime Coalition Cabinet. Between 1935 and 1939 he had visited Berlin and met Adolf Hitler and Rudolf Hess on numerous occasions. Hess regarded Baron Beaverbrook as an influential ally in Britain but was nervous of meeting him.

Hess's anxiety soon settled when Beaverbrook burst into his quarters on September 9th and stayed at his bedside for two hours. Full of charm and friendliness Beaverbrook approached 'Jonathan's' bed with an outstretched hand and a broad smile. Hess was soon eating out of his hand, relaxed and involved in animated conversation. They mainly discussed the threat Bolshevism presented to Germany and Britain. Hess was convinced world domination awaited the Soviet Union if her power was not broken and Britain should join with Germany immediately to ensure this did not happen. This discussion led inevitably for Rudolf Hess to outline Hitler's peace proposals. Baron Beaverbrook listened avidly and did not question Hess's statements and conclusions. He managed to convince the gullible Deputy Führer he was a potential convert to uphold Hitler's peace initiative.

After meeting Baron Beaverbrook Rudolf Hess was a changed man. Grinning cheerfully he told Captain Sutherland he had enjoyed his friend's company and he felt much better in himself. Hess was now ripe for the plucking but MI6 failed to press home their advantage. James had one fruitful session with 'Jonathan' three days after Baron Beaverbrook's visit. 'Jonathan' was behaving like an excited schoolboy and questioned James about his military training at Sandhurst and his involvement in the battle for France. James explained he was at the Guards Depot in Pirbright during the French campaign but his battalion was involved during the final days of the Dunkirk evacuation. At this point Rudolf Hess's face lit up with a supercilious grin and he asked a rhetorical question.

"Have you considered why so many British Tommy's escaped Dunkirk? Our armies could have wiped them out on the beaches. You have *Mein Führer*, Adolf Hitler, to thank for their survival. I was there when he ordered General von Runstedt's, Guderian's and Rommel's panzers to call a halt for three days to allow your troops to evacuate the beaches. This is proof, if you need proof, that *Mein Führer* wished to strike a peace deal with Britain and he agreed to my flying across to Scotland as a peace envoy." Hess stopped speaking abruptly as he realised he had probably gone too far. This revelation astounded James who declined to answer Jonathan. Hess's spontaneous outburst did not dampen his high spirits and he continued acting like a child concealing important secrets from an adoring parent for the rest of the day.

Largely due to Lord Beaverbrook's intervention Hess was allowed to read carefully edited weekly newssheets and to listen to news bulletins on the radio. Reports from Russian and North African battlefields came thick and fast during the last six months of 1941. German forces were sweeping forwards in both Theatres and 'Jonathan' was jubilant and ecstatic. His excitement gradually diminished at the beginning of October as the days with no response from the British Government passed by and Lord Beaverbrook's promises did not materialize. His depression returned with a bang on the 9th of October 1941. Major Foley informed 'Jonathan' his father, Fritz Hess, had died suddenly the previous day. Hess reacted with disbelief and demanded a meeting with the Swiss consul in London to verify the facts. His request was denied and, after a few days brooding, 'Jonathan' approached James.

"The Major told me my father is dead. I do not believe it. I want to go home to see my family. The Swiss consul in London will assist me. Will your Colonel see if he can arrange a meeting?"

"Yes, of course, *Herr Reichsminister*," James replied with no intention of adhering to the prisoner's request. This was the first of many attempts at repatriation Rudolf Hess made in captivity. British authorities took it for granted he would meet the fate ordered by Adolf Hitler after his ill-judged flight to Britain. If Hess set foot on German-occupied Europe he would be shot on sight and all his requests for medical repatriation were denied on these grounds.

James Sutherland was sitting with 'Jonathan' on the 7th of December 1941 when Japanese aircraft attacked Pearl Harbour and Roosevelt's declaration that America was at war with Japan. Rudolf Hess was puzzled but not overly concerned by the Japanese assault. He was, however, devastated when, three days later, Adolf Hitler declared war on the U.S.A. He sank into a deep, brooding depression and kept repeating, *"Nein, Nein."* 'Jonathan' had immediately recognised this turn of events might signal the end of the Third Reich and Adolf Hitler's ambition for world domination.

By March 1942, there was a complete change in the security staff at Camp Z. General Erwin Rommel's Panzers were on the rampage in Libya and driving Allied forces back towards Egypt and, by July, the Allies had dug a last-ditch defensive line at El Alamein, only sixty miles from Alexandria. Second Battalion Scots Guards were hurriedly deployed to North Africa as reinforcements for the 8th Army and with them went Captain James Sutherland and his Guards detachment. A succession of regimental line officers and a platoon from the Pioneer Corps replaced the Scots Guards. (The Pioneer Corps were regiments of the British Army during World War II). The turn-out and disciplinary standards of the "new" prison guards left a lot to be desired and Hess felt it was an insult to his rank as an SS Colonel General. He had developed a friendly, but correct, rapport with Captain James Sutherland but the new cadre Commanders were surly and unapproachable and frequent changes in command did little to help matters. This was the time when Hitler's armies were running riot in Russia and North Africa and Hess felt cheated he had no one to share his joy at Germany's conquests.

By March 1942 the Coalition Cabinet, in conjunction with MI6, had come to a conclusion Hess should be treated as a medical prisoner-of-war and would be more appropriately incarcerated in a psychiatric institution. Major Frank Foley left Mytchett Place to become head of MI5's Double-Cross Section in April 1942. He was completely disillusioned by Hess's grasp of the political and military situation in Nazi Germany and abandoned the Deputy Führer as a lost cause. It came as a relief to everyone at Camp Z to hear that the arrogant, psychotic Deputy Führer was to be transferred to a detention centre in Wales on the 25th of July 1942. The Pioneers travelled west with Rudolf Hess and continued to stand guard on the Deputy Führer for the thirty-eight months he was imprisoned at Maindiff Court Psychiatric and Military hospital in rural Monmouthshire.

MAINDIFF COURT HOSPITAL

25TH JULY 1942 – 10TH OCTOBER 1945

"Out of sight, out of mind" accurately describes Rudolf Hess's management by the authorities after July 1942. At Mytchett Place he had been a "one-day wonder", readily accessible for interrogation by military intelligence and Government agents from London, only 35 miles away. At Maindiff Court the atmosphere was more relaxed and casual and, though Hess was kept under "open arrest" for three years and three months, visits from central authorities were few and far apart. Ivone Kirkpatrick undertook irregular trips from London to keep an eye on the one-time prize prisoner. Dr N.R. Griffiths, the hospital's Superintendent, looked after Hess's day-to-day medical care and the resident psychiatrist, Major Ellis Jones, supervised his mental health which proved to be a major problem for the thirty-nine months Hess was incarcerated at Maindiff Court. The Pioneer Corps detachment had moved across from Camp Z in Mytchett en-bloc and supervised Hess's security at Maindiff.

Completed just before outbreak of World War II, Maindiff Court was a custom-built hospital for mentally challenged patients in South East Wales and situated at a rural location two miles north of Abergavenny. After the Dunkirk debacle in June 1940 the hospital was commandeered by the War Department for rehabilitation of battle casualties suffering from physical and mental trauma. A block in the south wing of the hospital, complete with its own wooded exercise compound, had been segregated from the main hospital, which was occupied by British battle casualties. Hess's quarters consisted of a lounge with French doors opening on to a lawn and exercise yard and a separate bedroom, bathroom and kitchen. To avoid any suicide attempts he was not allowed to cook in his kitchen and metal utensils were not provided in his cellblock. Three meals a day, mostly vegetarian fare, were brought to his sitting room at set times and, if requested, he was allowed a glass of wine, or whisky, with his evening meal. Writing, painting and reading materials were freely provided and he was allowed to listen to BBC news bulletins most nights. Two Pioneer Corps guards were permanently stationed at the entrance corridor leading to Hess's cellblock and another two patrolled for 24 hours a day outside the barbed wire fence enclosing the lawn and exercise compound.

When he was mentally alert, and accompanied by an armed Pioneer guard or the Guard Commander, Rudolf Hess made full use of his exercise breaks each morning and evening. They were mostly conducted in strict silence. The Deputy Führer was remarkably agile for his age and walked rapidly with a strutting action often leaving the accompanying guards trailing behind in his wake. In his cellblock Hess spent his time reading historical novels, listening to operatic music, sketching and water colouring. He was allowed to write one censored letter home every two months, carefully censored to avoid revealing his whereabouts in Britain. By the end of 1942 he was regularly driven in a duty station wagon on local outings to the surrounding countryside and into Abergavenny town on market days.

Monmouthshire abounds with castles and White Castle, near Abergavenny, was his favourite spot where he spent hours sketching and painting. During the summer months Hess was frequently seen walking and sketching on the banks of the River Usk and, allegedly, drinking a glass of tepid beer at the Walnut Tree Inn, a mile away from Maindiff Court. Occasionally he was entertained to lunch at the White House in Llanfoist, the Hospital Commandant's private quarters during the war. Abergavenny's inhabitants were fully aware of his true identity and were accustomed to seeing Rudolf Hess, and his accompanying bodyguards, in the town and its environs. For reasons of wartime security he was always referred to by the locals as "The Kaiser".

Rudolf Hess's term of incarceration at Mytchett Place and Maindiff Court was plagued by frequent bouts of mental instability, depression and amnesia. In 1943 the fortunes of the Nazi war machine were being sorely tested on the Russian front and by the joint British and American assault on Rommel's Africa Crops in Tunisia. Unfavourable news bulletins came with regular frequency and were sufficient to hurl Hess into fits of depression. The attempt on Hitler's life in July 1944 threw him into the doldrums for a fortnight. His mental aberrations did not follow a routine pattern. A minor incident at Maindiff Court, such as overhearing a guard refer to the Führer as a 'bastard', would start off days of depression and paranoia, mainly directed against Jews. His reactions were typical examples of a neurotic patient with a long history of mental instability and a devotee of astronomy, holistic medicine and the mystical occult. In his mentally unstable state Hess was consumed with paranoia and convinced someone, usually Jewish, was poisoning his food or drink. Consequently he often refused to eat his meals unless someone tasted the food first. He complained of disturbed sleep due to nocturnal noises. A busy railway junction, half a mile away from Maindiff Court, was a constant source for complaints at night and he blamed these disturbances on the Jews. Rudolf Hess's psychosomatic symptoms were exacerbated during depressive episodes – stomach cramps, excruciating headaches, chest and kidney pains and constipation. 'Jonathan' refused tablets and injections insisting only on taking herbal medicines. To cap this gamut of psychological claptrap he frequently reverted to real, or imagined, amnesia even to the extent of forgetting the Führer's name and his previous involvement with the Nazi Party.

During his months of incarceration Rudolf Hess was examined by a host of psychiatrists and they all came to a conclusion he was not insane. They differed, however, in their evaluation as to the cause of his mental instability. It was agreed he suffered from depression and paranoia and other diagnoses varied from schizophrenia to depressive psychosis. R.A.M.C. Major Ellis Jones attended and observed Hess at Maindiff Court for three-and-a-half years and his opinion of Hess's mental state is the most reliable account available. The Major concluded Rudolf Hess was a paranoid depressive. His main obsession was that he was surrounded by Jewish secret agents who were out to poison him, or to poison his mind, in an attempt to make him insane. These secret agents allegedly made deliberate noises at night to interrupt his sleep and to annoy him. In his manic fantasies Hess behaved with haughty arrogance but his mood swings often culminated in childish outbursts. The periods of amnesia exhibited by Hess from time to time served to complicate his unorthodox mental reactions and, as the months wore on, his frequent inability to remember events in the past became a puzzling problem to the psychiatric experts.

Major Ellis Jones and Rudolf Hess developed a strictly

correct doctor/patient relationship at Maindiff Court, unlike the friendly bond he had forged with Captain James Sutherland at Mytchett Place. Successive guard commanders at Maindiff were aggressive and antagonistic and seemingly displeased by their secondment from regimental duties and possible promotion. The main body of Pioneer Corps guards were dull and boorish and, with the exception of two, a corporal and a private, were completely disinterested in the Nazi prisoner. Corporal David White from London, called Chalky White by his peers, and Private Joseph Clancy from Manchester had been seconded to the Pioneer Corps from their line regiments and, between April and July 1942, they were on guard duty at Camp Z in Mytchett. They were then transferred en-bloc across to Maindiff Court to continue guarding Rudolf Hess and, after a few months, the "Kaiser" came to recognise their presence. The two worked as a team, in contrast to the main body of Pioneers on guard duty at Maindiff Court. When Hess felt in the mood for conversation he elected to speak with Corporal Chalky and Private Joey who were always polite and courteous and provided the Deputy Führer with local Camp gossip and the most recent reports on the wars' progress on all Fronts.

At a conference in Casablanca in January 1943 U.S. President Franklin D. Roosevelt and British Prime Minister Winston Churchill agreed to demand unconditional surrender from Germany at the end of World War II. Ten months later they met again at Tehran on two occasions, and USSR dictator Joseph Stalin, was present at both meetings. Secret discussions took place on the fate of the Nazi leaders at conclusion of hostilities in Europe and a list of culpable Nazis was compiled. Rudolf Hess's name was included in the top ten war criminals. Uncle Joe Stalin was adamant all the top Nazi leaders and SS officers should be executed without trial. On his return to Whitehall Churchill informed Clement Attlee and the War Cabinet about the existence of this "list" and Stalin's insistence they should all be shot. Attlee, and the majority of the Cabinet, was in favour of clemency for Rudolf Hess, arguing he was a medical casualty and he had served his time for any war crimes he had committed as Deputy Führer before the war. Joseph Stalin, on the other hand, believed Hess was the chief organizer of Operation Barbarossa which had caused the death of millions of his countrymen. The Prime Minister knew this not to be true and, if Stalin got his way, the Deputy Führer would be certain to face an execution squad. Winston Churchill himself was edging towards clemency for Rudolf Hess and, with Attlee and the Cabinet's approval, he ordered MI6 to investigate the feasibility of sheltering Hess at the end of hostilities and his possible replacement with an impostor. Such a plan appealed to Churchill's scheming nature and would kill two birds with one stone. Firstly, it would placate Clement Attlee and his Cabinet colleagues and, secondly, it would be a slap in the face for Joseph Stalin, Russia's ruthless dictator. The proposed plans for a 'switch' now assumed a certain degree of priority at MI6.

The 2nd Battalion Scots Guards played a major role in the 8th Army's defeat of Rommel's Africa Corps in April 1943. Major James Sutherland, now a Company Commander, was actively involved at El Alamein and the subsequent advance of Montgomery's 'Desert Rats' into Tunisia. The Scots Guards then took part in Allied landings on the Italian mainland at Salerno in September 1943. Promoted Lieutenant Colonel in November, Sutherland was recalled to Britain to take command of the 3rd Battalion Scots Guards based at Aldershot and training in preparation for the cross-channel invasion of Nazi-occupied

Europe in June 1944.

Ivone Kirkpatrick made irregular visits to check on Hess at Maindiff Court. The Nazi prisoner still bore a grudge against him, and the British Government, for not accepting Hitler's peace proposals in May 1941. Hess's demands for repatriation had been constantly denied on the grounds that Adolf Hitler had ordered his summary execution if he ever set foot on Nazi-occupied territory. Kirkpatrick realised that if the plan to 'protect' Hess at the end of the war had any prospects of succeeding MI6 would require his full cooperation. Fully aware Hess had established a friendly rapport with James Sutherland at Mytchett Place in 1941, arrangements were made by MI6 for the Guards' Lieutenant Colonel to meet up with the one-time Deputy Führer at Maindiff Court.

Lieutenant Colonel Sutherland turned up unexpectedly at Maindiff Court on a blustery St David's Day, March the 1st, 1944. In one of his saner moods, Rudolf Hess welcomed him like a long-lost friend with a warm smile and a firm handshake. Playfully he tapped the crown on James's shoulder and murmured,

"Mein Gott!, Herr Colonel!, Mein Gott!"

Despite a chilly wind Hess insisted they should stroll together on the lawn outside his cellblock. Wrapped in greatcoats and scarves they walked side by side across the compound and Hess did most of the questioning. He showed an interest in James's war up to date and the Scots Guards officer saw no reason why he should not tell him about the North African campaign. James was complimentary about Field Marshal Rommel's battle strategies and fair treatment of British casualties and prisoners-of-war. Hess responded, "General Erwin Rommel is the best Commander in our Army. He is far superior to any of those Prussian generals in the Wehrmacht. I got on well with *Herr* General Rommel."

James then described the action at the Salerno landings on the Italian mainland in September 1943 and mentioned Italy's surrender to the Allies the same month. Hess's mood changed abruptly. He scowled and stared at James.

"The traitor Mussolini stabbed *Mein Führer* in the back. He always was a bag full of wind. The Italian army are not brave. They declared war on us after *Mein Faterland* helped them out in Greece and North Africa."

Rudolf Hess was visibly upset and the two walked twice around the lawn in complete silence with the armed Pioneer corporal trailing twenty yards behind. James broke the ice." *Herr Reichsminister*! Assuming the Allies win, what do you think will happen to yourself at the end of the war?"

Hess pulled up sharply.

"Britain will not win the war. But if they do I will return to Germany and help *Mein Führer* rebuild the Third Reich."

"I fear you will not be allowed to do that. There will be a Tribunal and the Russians are already demanding reparations," James retorted. Rudolf Hess looked vacantly into space.

"In that case I will sacrifice my life for the Fatherland. At least I shall be allowed to lay at rest beside *Mein Führer*."

The interview was coming to an end. James explored one further avenue.

"The British Government can arrange to spare your life if you so wish. Are you prepared to give it consideration?"

Hess stopped in his tracks and paused for half a minute.

"Yes. I am prepared to listen -- but Britain must win the war first," and then, with a shrug and a smile, he asked cheekily, "When do you intend invading us?"

It was James's turn to stop walking and to respond with a sheepish grin.

"I don't know Sir, and if I did, I cannot tell you, *Herr Reichsminister.*"

Later the same day Lieutenant Sutherland reported back to MI6.

"If we play our cards right the prisoner at Maindiff may well cooperate and be amenable to suggestions."

Lieutenant Sutherland's 3rd Battalion Scots Guards landed in Normandy on D. Day plus six and were deployed in fierce fighting at Caen. His battalion then took part in the Allied advance northwards through France and Belgium and, at the beginning of September 1944, the Scots Guards were dug-in on the outskirts of Hertogenbosh in southern Holland. During a heavy bombardment by German artillery a shell splinter shattered James's left hip. Evacuated by air to a military hospital in Cambridge, his hip joint was fused and he was bedridden on traction for three months. By mid-January 1945 James was ambulant again but walked with a pronounced limp and with the aid of a walking stick. A Medical Board considered him unfit for front line duty and he was seconded to the Ministry of Defence in Whitehall in the first week in February 1945 as a liaison officer with MI6. MI6 agents were located in a labyrinth of subterranean cellars at the M.O.D. building and, within days of his arrival, James Sutherland was co-opted into a group of agents investigating the thorny problem of what to do with Rudolf Hess at cessation of hostilities and the possibility of replacing him with an impostor.

The future outlook for Hess changed dramatically in July 1945. At a general election Clement Attlee's Labour Party swept into power at Westminster. Within days of becoming Prime

Minister Attlee ordered the head of MI6, Sir Stewart Menzies, to urgently implement any plans for safeguarding Rudolf Hess from the probability of execution should he come to Trial. Ten days after becoming Britain's post-war Prime Minister, Attlee flew to Potsdam for a meeting with Joseph Stalin and the new U.S. President, Harry S. Truman. The fate for the top Nazis was discussed and Hess's name was included high on the list of war criminals indicted to appear for trial. Attlee kept his cards close to his chest. He was in full agreement with plans to shield Rudolf Hess from trial for war crimes and contrived not to divulge his secret knowledge to other participants at the conference. There is little doubt that Churchill had advised President Roosevelt before he died of a proposed 'switch' but Harry S Truman was a "new boy on the block" and had more important concerns on his mind. The atomic bomb attacks on Japan, which brought World War II to an end, claimed priority and it is doubtful if the President was fully aware of the implications of a 'switch' to save Hess from the gallows. It is equally likely that he delegated Rudolf Hess's future fate to Prime Minister Attlee, the British Cabinet and MI6.

PLANNING THE "SWITCH"

FEBRUARY 1945 – 10 OCTOBER 1945

As the war in Europe progressed to its inevitable conclusion in the spring of 1945, Rudolf Hess's mental condition continued to cause major concerns to the authorities. His mounting depressive episodes were complicated by long periods of imagined, or real, amnesia and they continued to be a subject for debate among psychiatric clinicians. His amnesia waxed and waned and was largely dependent on war bulletins and progress of the Russian armies approaching Berlin. On the 14th of February 1945, the "Kaiser of Abergavenny" made a second feeble attempt to take his own life. He stabbed himself twice in the chest with a bread knife. The superficial puncture wounds were barely skin deep and only required half a dozen sutures. Afterwards Hess claimed he had no memory of the incident though, later on, he said he did it to fool the doctors at Maindiff Court.

Adolf Hitler committed suicide in the Führerbunker under the Reichschancellery in Berlin at 3 p.m. on the 30th of April 1945. At first Hess refused to accept his master and idol had taken his own life in this manner. A few days later he learnt that Eva Braun, Hitler's bride of barely 36 hours, and his dog Blondi, had suffered the same fate. Hess withdrew into his shell and spoke to no one for over a week. News that Dr Joseph Göebbels' wife and six children had committed suicide on the day before the Führer's death made no impression on Hess and neither did Admiral Karl Döenitz's surrender of Germany to the Western

Allies at Luneberg Heath on the 8th of May 1945.

Hess emerged from his melancholic abyss at the end of May. The medical staff at Maindiff Court detected a sense of despair and failure in his demeanour, which gradually gave way to guilt because he had been denied his wish to die alongside his beloved Führer. A seed of self-preservation was sown in Hess's mind and he developed fantasies of becoming Germany's post-war saviour, and Leader, resurrecting a new Third Reich from the ashes. He imagined he would be of greater value alive to his *Herrenvolk* as a messiah to take over where the Führer left off. The main stumbling block to his grandiose aims to resurrect Germany were the Communists and European Jewry and, for further advancement of his perceived destiny, he agreed to cooperate with the British authorities. Hess assumed he would be able to direct his plans for Germany from a position in exile. MI6 agents made frequent visits to Maindiff Court during the turbulent months following the end of hostilities in Europe and, by June 1945, they were convinced that Rudolf Hess was ready to 'strike a deal' with the British Government. They pressed ahead urgently on plans to secure his future.

On July 17th 1945, Lieutenant Colonel James Sutherland attended a briefing at MI6 headquarters in Whitehall, chaired by Ivone Kirkpatrick and Sir Stewart Menzies, head of MI6, sitting on his right hand side, made the opening remarks.

"Our new PM at Number 10 has ordered MI6 to make every effort to replace the Nazi prisoner at Maindiff with an impostor. All attempts to get 'Jonathan' off his indictment on psychiatric grounds have failed and the Kremlin insists that he must appear at a War Crimes Tribunal in Nuremberg, scheduled to convene in mid- October. This gives us 10 weeks to prepare the ground. The Department has already pinpointed four possible impostors in Germany but we have no certain knowledge whether they are dead or alive. 'Jonathan' is coming around to the idea of cooperating with us but he does not altogether trust our Department. He has faith in you, Colonel Sutherland. It may be a nonstarter but we must attempt to find a compliant impostor. Your task will be to identify and train a person to represent 'Jonathan' at a War Crimes Tribunal. Any questions Colonel Sutherland?"

"What will be the prisoner's fate if I fail to find a stand-in?"

"In that case 'Jonathan' will be sent to Nuremberg to stand trial and I leave the end result to your imagination," Kirkpatrick replied and handed James a typed dossier marked 'Top Secret'.

"This will provide up-to-date information on the possible stand-ins you will need to investigate urgently."

Sir Stewart Menzies summed up the briefing. "My Department has been given the responsibility of organizing this 'switch'. Its implementation carries an A.1. top priority, rating. We rely on you, James, to leave no stone unturned to unearth a suitable impostor. My Department, and the PM, depend on your ability to replace the prisoner at Maindiff Court with a reliable and trustworthy stand-in."

James Sutherland promised to do his utmost best to fulfil the assignment.

Lieutenant Colonel Sutherland flew to Gatow airfield in Berlin on the 20th of July 1945, at the very time Prime Minister Attlee was at a Three-Power conference at Potsdam. MI6 researchers had discovered that, between 1934 and 1941, Rudolf Hess had employed at least four regular stand-in lookalikes. An earlier stand-in in Munich was considerably older than Hess and now suffered from total baldness, and a second had been reported killed in a road traffic accident at Hanover in 1942. The third, and most promising, prospect was a part-time actor who had been regularly employed as a stand-in for Hess. His name was Ernst Prost but MI6 had no up-to-date information about his current whereabouts and if, in fact, he was still alive. On the fourth candidate they only had sketchy information and none since October 1938. The obvious target for James was Ernest Prost, last reported to have been seen in the Kufurstendam area of Berlin at Christmastime 1944.

At the end of hostilities in Europe the hastily set-up British Sector of Berlin was an enclave inside the Russian dominated Zone of East Berlin. Within its barbed wire boundaries the British Sector included the Brandenburg Gate, a mile stretch of Kufurstendam Strasse and the Havel and Charlottenburg districts. Allied bombing raids and Russian shelling had reduced most of the city's buildings to shadowy shells of heaped-up, jagged rubble. Side roads were blocked by tons of bricks and shell craters and most streets were cut off completely to motorized traffic. Main roads were unlit at night and only important road and rail junctions and bus stations were lit by temporary lighting. Desperate Berliners scrambled among the piles of rubble, foraging for food and looting damaged properties. British Military Police, the Redcaps, were in evidence during the day making futile attempts to control the desperate civilians. After dark there were a few military check points at major road junctions but, otherwise, Berlin was wide open to pilfering vagrants and armed gangs roamed the darkened streets seemingly robbing, looting and raping at will.

James knew the address, just off the Kudam, where Prost had been employed up until Christmas 1944 and a uniformed Military Policeman drove him at midday to the centre of Berlin. All allied military personnel in West Berlin were required to wear a uniform at all times in public but Sutherland was dressed in civilian clothes. The building he was looking for was in a cratered side street just a hundred yards from the Kufurstendam Strasse. Miraculously three large houses stood out starkly amid piles of rubble, two with their roofs missing and the third apparently intact and with a naked red light bulb hanging in the porch. This was the target brothel James had in mind to pay a call.

The splintered, cracked wooden door swung open in response to James' knocking and a plump, bottle-blonde Frau invited him to follow her into a dimly lit lounge crammed with tattered leather sofas. Directly under a naked light bulb at the far end sat another blousy blonde clutching a glass of schnapps and scribbling figures on a notepad. Carrying his walking stick James limped across the floor towards the seated harridan and greeted her in German.

"Wie gehts mein gnedige Frau?"

The formidable blonde looked up suspiciously and glanced at a grandfather clock standing in the corner.

"You are too early for the girls. Business starts here at two o'clock. What do you want?"

"Is Ernst Prost still working here?" James asked. The madam screwed up her eyes and inclined her head.

"Who wants to know?" she asked.

"I have some good news for Ernst," James replied. The grim-faced, heavy-jowled Frau shook her head. James delved into his overcoat pocket and produced a tin of Nescafe and two packets of Players cigarettes. The madam's eyes reflected her greed and her rasping, throaty voice had convinced James she was a heavy smoker. Real coffee and cigarettes were like liquid gold in post-war Germany and of greater bartering value than the virtually bankrupt Reichsmark.

"Ernst Prost did work for me as a doorman until January. The Russians were coming and he left here in a great hurry. He said he was going to Hamburg to look for work in the Reeperbhan district. That's all I know."

She made a lunge for a cigarette packet and James stood up to leave. The blonde madam lit a cigarette, inhaled deeply, and sat back in her chair with an ecstatic smile on her face. As James reached the lounge door she gave a rasping cough and shouted in his direction.

"You won't have any trouble finding Prost. He is so frightened he looks like the Nazi Hess he wears a black coat and hat and dark glasses day and night. For all I know he keeps glasses on in bed!"

As James left the brothel he could hear the blousy madam chuckling and laughing at her own joke.

James Sutherland left Berlin the next day and was driven in an army truck to Hamburg, a slow journey which took nearly five hours along shell-cratered roads. The devastation in Germany's main seaport was similar, if not more prolific, than in Berlin. Allied aerial bombing, and the firebomb raids in July 1943, had virtually reduced the City centre to a pile of rubble. The Red Light District in the Reeperbhan had not escaped lightly and the cratered, gutted streets were draped with derelict, blackened and fractured buildings.

On the night of his arrival in Hamburg James paid a visit to the Reeperbhan. Three "reputable" brothels were open for business and outside the second one. James came across a black-hatted, black-coated doorman wearing dark glasses. In order not to scare him away, James pretended to be a timid customer wondering if he could afford to entry to the brothel. He sidled up to the doorman.

"How much is entry?" he asked in German.

"You pay me 100 marks. Inside a girl will cost you 500 marks," the doorman in black replied.

"*Danke*. I don't have enough money. Will you accept coffee or cigarettes instead?"

Assuming the well-dressed stranger was a racketeer the man in black faced-up to James and answered with a cheeky smirk.

"*Jawhol, mein Herr.*"

James produced a tin of Nescafe and a cigarette packet. The greedy doorman pocketed the gifts and, standing aside, ordered James to follow him into the brothel. James wavered and pretended he was still undecided if he had the courage to enter the lion's den. The man in black came close to him and whispered,

"Two packets of cigarettes will get you a girl for one hour."

James stared straight into his dark glasses.

"I am not interested in girls. I have good news for a man called Ernst Prost. Does he work here?"

The man behind the dark glasses showed no emotion.

"I might be able to help but it will cost you. Come back here at three o'clock when I get off duty. We will discuss costs then and bring more cigarettes. Is that agreed?"

"*Jawhol mein Her*," James Sutherland replied and took his leave certain he had identified the right person. Back in the army barracks he sent a cablegram to MI6.

'Made contact with target. Hopeful for a result. Will fly into 'nest' on Thursday or Friday. J. S.'

The 'nest' mentioned in the cablegram was Camp Z in Mytchett, Rudolf Hess's prison for the first fourteen months of his incarceration in Britain.

Promptly at 3:00am the man in black emerged from the

brothel. James was waiting in a doorway across the street. Joining forces, and without speaking, they wandered down the dark, deserted Reeperbhan and, within 200 yards, they turned into a short side street which led into Prinz Albers Plaz. The brothel concierge looked each way up and down the square and then scurried down a flight of steps into the basement of a bomb-shattered house, closely followed by James. The single-roomed cellar was dark and damp and smelt of mildew, stale food and Jeyes fluid detergent. The doorman lit a candle and, in the dim light, he turned to face James Sutherland.

"Who are you and what do you want with me?"

Sitting at a grease-stained, rickety, wooden table James was prepared for the question.

"I have come from England to find Ernst Prost and I was hoping you could help me. Prost may be of service to *Reichsminister* Rudolf Hess who has been a prisoner in our care for four years. He has asked me to find out if Prost can carry out a mission on his behalf. If you can help me to get in touch with Prost you will be well-compensated," and James placed four cigarette packets and half a bottle of Napoleon brandy on the fat-stained table. At the mention of Hess the man in black sprang to attention, clicked his heels, and made a conscious effort to stop himself flinging out his right arm in a Nazi salute. He took off his black Trilby and dark glasses and announced proudly,

"I am Ernst Prost. I will do anything to be of service to Reichsführer Rudolf Hess. What do you wish me to do?"

James sat staring at Prost, mesmerized by his facial likeness to the 'real' Hess. Pleased with Prost's response James explained.

"You will need to come to England with me to meet Rudolf

Hess and there everything will be explained to you. Do you agree to go with me?"

Ernst Prost was already a worried man. He had foreseen that to remain in Germany he ran a grave risk of imprisonment or, at worst, execution if he was apprehended by the Russians. The British were offering him a safety line and Prost's response was immediate.

"There is nothing for me here in Hamburg but trouble. I am prepared and eager to leave and meet *Mein Reichsführer*."

James almost jumped for joy. He had secured an impostor without undue difficulty

"We leave for England in four hours' time. I'll pick you up outside Cafe Schwarzwald on the Reeperbhan. Do not tell anyone you are leaving and do not bring any personal belongings with you. Just leave your flat in the state that it is in. You will be provided with everything you need."

"What is your name *mein Herr*?" Prost queried.

"Just call me Jim," Sutherland replied.

Still dressed in black and wearing dark glasses, Ernst Prost arrived outside Cafe Schwarzwald at the appointed hour. He did not carry a suitcase and the only objects in his coat pocket were three cigarette packs and a replica Nazi Party membership medallion No.16 presented to Prost by Hess at a Nuremberg Party Rally in 1937. The half bottle of Napoleon brandy had been consumed during the night. Prost sat in the back of an army staff car with the man he knew as 'Jim' by his side. They were driven to Hamburg's temporary airstrip outside the city and, three and a half hours later, they landed on English soil at Biggin Hill. A further car journey saw them arrive at Camp Z at 6:30pm on the 24th of July. Ernst Prost was deliberately installed in the very quarters Rudolf Hess had occupied after his fateful flight to Scotland in May 1941. The readiness with which Prost had agreed to cross the Channel, and accepted the restriction of virtual imprisonment at Camp Z, astounded James Sutherland. Ernst Prost was ecstatic when he was told his Nazi idol spent fourteen months of his imprisonment in England in the very same cellblock he was occupying at Mytchett Place.

Ernst Prost was a complex character. He was born in August 1895 at a Catholic Hostel for Fallen Women in Cologne and adopted at birth by a middle-class family in Munich. His surrogate father, Joseph Prost, ran a successful butchery business in the city centre and infant Ernst was destined to become his sole heir. The Prost's were informed by the Catholic nuns that Ernst's mother came from a wealthy family in Franconia. As a boy Ernst was well educated and spoke fluent German and passable French and English, but he lacked academic application at school and dreamt of a career on the stage. At the outbreak of World War I he enlisted in the German army and spent the entire war at a supply depot in Maastricht. Slightly effeminate, he became a popular member of a base camp theatrical party, frequently called upon to perform female roles. After demobilization in January 1919 Ernst returned to Munich to work in his father's butchery business.

Ernst was a 'loner' and never married. His uncanny likeness to Rudolf Hess came into prominence in November 1924 when Hess and Hitler were incarcerated at Landsberg prison after the Beer Hall Putsch fiasco. At that time Hitler was a Music Hall joke and the object of derision in amateur vaudeville sketches. At local beer halls and theatres Ernst was portrayed as the Führer's fawning handmaid, hovering in the background and snuggling-up to the Chaplinesque character playing the part of Adolf Hitler.

Ernst Prost's adopted parents were tragically killed in a skiing accident in 1928 and, within a year, Ernst sold his father's butchery business to concentrate on a career in vaudeville. In 1932 Martin Bormann, at that time Hess's private secretary at the Braunhaus in Munich, saw Prost's vaudeville act and immediately enlisted him as a stand-in for Hess. Prost first stood-in for his master at the annual Nuremberg Party Rally in September 1935. Hess made an impassioned introduction to present the Führer to the assembled masses. One hour into the parade that followed Hitler's address, Hess left the saluting base and, within twenty minutes, he was replaced by Ernst Prost. None of the Nazi Party bigwigs, including Adolf Hitler, noticed the 'switch'. Martin Bormann was the only top Nazi on the saluting base "in" on the deception. Pleased with the success of the enterprise Bormann revealed the scam to Hitler who ordered him to employ Prost as one of Hess's permanent substitutes.

In his new position Ernst was able to study his subject at close quarters and to adopt Hess's speaking voice, accents and pauses, his peculiar manly, strutting gait and his intimate mannerisms. Between 1933 and 1941 he was at Bormann's beck and call and stood-in for the "real" Hess on umpteen occasions. Due to Prost's striking similarity to the Deputy Führer he was immediately recognisable in public and, for his own protection, he either wore a black felt hat or a dark-blue military-style cap and dark glasses whenever he was out of doors. For the majority of Germans Ernst Prost on stage became Rudolf Hess and he himself began to believe in the harshness of the Treaty of Versailles, the threat from Jews and Communists and the need for 'lebensraum' for the German herrenvolk.

Ernst Prost's privileged life-style fell to pieces on the 10th of May 1941 when his lord and master absconded to Britain and he became a persona-non-grata with the Party leaders. Martin Bormann immediately dismissed him and advised he should disappear from view and volunteer to serve on the Eastern Front. Prost took the first part of Bormann's advice and slunk into the seedy nightlife of Berlin's wartime bordellos. An attempted revival of his pre-war sketches fell afoul of the Gestapo in 1944 and he was imprisoned for six months for subversive activities against the State. Despite persecution from the Politzei and Gestapo he kept faith with the Party and with Rudolf Hess and the Führer. The mere mention of the Deputy Führer rekindled vivid memories of his glory days when he truly believed he was performing a valuable service for the Nazi Party and the Third Reich.

By December 1944 Prost had been reduced to holding a poorly paid job as a concierge at a Berlin brothel. To camouflage his identity he constantly wore a long, black overcoat, black Trilby hat and dark glasses. Failure to do so would probably lead to instant recognition and physical abuse largely generated by the fact the Police, the Gestapo and Berliners were obsessed by Göebbels's propaganda accusing Hess of desertion in May 1941. Ernst Prost refused to believe his master was a deserter and, when the opportunity came in July 1945 to cross to England and meet Rudolf Hess again, he jumped at the chance without hesitation. Prost was also fully aware that should he remain in Germany, and fall into Russian hands, his prospects of survival were extremely slim.

James Sutherland, by now a full-blown MI6 agent, had barely three months to prepare Prost for his proposed assignment. The impostor's first month in England was deliberately spent at Mytchett Place, to accustom him to the surroundings Hess encountered when he first landed on British soil. He was shown the cell in the Tower of London, where Hess spent five days expecting to be executed as a spy. For authenticity he was placed under house arrest and guarded by a detachment of Scots Guards and a cadre from the Pioneer Corps. It soon became apparent that nothing needed to be done on Prost's physical transformation. He was a 'dead-ringer' for the "Kaiser of Abergavenny". Attention was needed to his lifestyle and his responses to stress under interrogation. The services of an army psychiatrist was enrolled to instruct Prost on how to feign amnesia and depression and how to express concern that his food was poisoned and he was being persecuted by the Jews. Rudolf Hess's vegetarian dietary habits were spartan and he was a virtual teetotaller. On the other hand, Ernst Prost was a habitual smoker, a heavy drinker and, as a butcher's son, a hearty carnivore whenever meat was available. For a month at Camp Z Prost's dietary, alcoholic and smoking habits were strictly controlled and by the end of August 1945 he had virtually become a non-smoking, non-drinking vegetarian.

James Sutherland took great care to improve Prost's English vocabulary and to replicate Rudolf Hess's handwriting. If Prost was to take over Hess's identity another complication presented itself. At Maindiff Court, in February 1945, Hess made a second farcical attempt at suicide by stabbing himself twice with a bread knife on the left side of his chest. The stab wounds were superficial and only required a few stitches. For authenticity Prost agreed to undergo the same procedure under local anaesthetic leaving him with two fresh, one-inch scars on his left chest. Prost endured all these sacrifices without complaint and, all the while, he kept asking when, and where, he would meet the one time Deputy Führer.

By the end of August 1945 Ernst was convinced he would never meet up with his Nazi idol. MI6 officers hedged their replies by quoting "soon" and "very soon". Prost had developed a trustworthy rapport with James Sutherland during the five weeks they had spent together at Camp Z and he insisted James should be present when he was interviewed on the 28th of August by an MI6 panel chaired by Sir Stewart Menzies, the MI6 supremo. Menzies and Ivone Kirkpatrick questioned Prost for an hour on his connections in the Nazi Party and his contacts with Rudolf Hess. Sir Stewart Menzies then came to the chief purpose of their meeting.

"*Herr* Prost! What are you prepared to do for *Reichsminister* Hess?"

Prost stiffened in his chair.

"I will do anything for my Deputy Führer. I will even give my life for him if necessary."

"Will you be able to stand trial on behalf of your Deputy Führer?"

Without hesitation Ernst Prost replied:

"It would be an honour."

This was exactly the answer the MI6 panel wanted to hear.

"You will have to persuade the *Reichsminister* to allow you to enter the witness box on his behalf. The court may pass a death sentence on you. Are you still prepared to go ahead?"

Ernst Prost simply replied, "Yes," and glanced at Sutherland who nodded his approval and spoke up for the first time.

"You will be at liberty to disclose your identity to the Court at any time. They will have no option but to release you as a free man. Is that understood *Herr* Prost?"

"Yes, of course, *Herr* Colonel. What will happen to *mein* Deputy Führer?"

Sir Stewart Menzies smiled and answered.

"Herr Rechsminister will be in a secret hideout long before the trial begins. You have our word on that."

Prost lowered his head slightly and spoke, almost in a whisper. "Thank God for that" and, on impulse, his body stiffened again and he clicked his heels under the table.

On his return journey from Camp Z to London Sir Stewart Menzies discussed plans for a 'switch' between Hess and an impostor with Ivon Kirkpartrick and concluded with a statement. "I am confident we have all the main ingredients for a successful 'switch' at Maindiff Court. I will advise the PM that we are ready to proceed. 'Jonathan' is due to be transported to Nuremberg in the second week in October. Agent Sutherland will now take the impostor to South Wales to meet Hess and fix the 'switch'. We will work on 'Jonathan's' documentation and transfer out of Britain at this end. I see no reason why this will not work."

Two days after the meeting at Camp Z James Sutherland took an overnight train to Newport in South Wales and was transported by staff car to Maindiff Court Hospital. He was accompanied to Rudolf Hess's quarters by Lieutenant Colonel Jefferys, the hospital Commandant. James hobbled into Hess's cellblock unannounced and was greeted by the prisoner with a warm smile of recognition.

"Why the stick, *mein* Colonel?"

James smiled in return.

"A little accident, *Herr Reichsminister.*"

Hess then turned his attention to the hospital Commandant whom he obviously disliked and asked with a suspicious glare.

"What is going on?"

James read the signs and dismissed the Commandant and

the Pioneer guards. He invited Hess to take a stroll around the exercise compound. It was a hot summer's day but Hess insisted on wearing a green pullover. James asked if Hess had any complaints. Hess stopped striding and pulled up abruptly. Inclining his head, he glanced towards the open French door in his cellblock.

"The Commandant is not cooperative and I think the hospital cook is a Jew and he's out to poison me."

This was a persistent complaint and James made no comment. They started off at pace again until they reached the furthest point in the compound.

"Your trial is fixed *Herr Reichsminister*. You and twenty-two of your colleagues are indicted to appear for war crimes."

Rudolf continued striding ahead and replied.

"I am ready to appear and I will defend myself. My only wish is to restore Germany's rightful place in the world after the shameful treatment we received from France and Britain at Versailles in 1918."

He then fell silent and continued walking with his stilted gait. James Sutherland was not surprised the arrogant Nazi prisoner had taken this stance. After all was said and done, Hess still considered he was a force to be reckoned with in Germany and he had sacrificed his liberty, and paid the penalty, by flying to negotiate a peace settlement with Britain in 1941. James decided to shock Rudolf Hess.

"The Russian advocates have asked for a death penalty for all twenty-three on trial."

Again, Hess did not stop striding and replied:

"What will be, will be. I am ready to die for the Fatherland."

They did a full circuit on the exercise compound. Jonathan was lost in deep thought until James broke the silence.

"I met you here in March last year and you agreed to consider suggestions to spare your life. Does that promise still hold water, *Herr Reichsminister?*"

Hess stopped walking and glared directly at James. After a minute's consideration he replied.

"I did make a promise and I am open to suggestion."

James Sutherland pressed on with his advantage.

"Ernst Prost is over here in England. He has expressed a wish to see you. Will you see him?"

At the mention of Prost, Hess's normally stern and blank face broke into a broad smile.

"Prost is a good German and a loyal Party member. He was employed in my Department at the Braunhaus in Munich in the thirties. I will be pleased to meet him again."

"It will be arranged, *Herr Reichsminister,*" Sutherland replied. The Scots Guard's MI6 agent then took his leave and returned by train to London. Satisfied with Rudolf Hess's offer of cooperation James Sutherland reported back to MI6 and was given the green light to go ahead and fix the 'switch'.

Gliffaes is a country hotel perched on a wooded promontory overlooking the majestic river Usk, two miles outside Crickhowell and eleven miles along tortuous secondary roads and country lanes from Maindiff Court Hospital. In 1945 the hotel was requisitioned as an Officers' Mess for military personnel in training on Brecon Beacons and, for five weeks, Lieutenant Colonel James Sutherland and Ernst Prost were billeted in a segregated private bungalow at the rear of the hotel. Driven by an R.A.S.C. corporal, MI6 agent Barlow, James Sutherland and *Herr* Prost made the three-hour journey from Mytchett Place to Gliffaes hotel on the 1st of September 1945. MI6 had made arrangements for a surprise visit to Rudolf Hess at 11:00 pm on the following day.

Corporal Chalky White and Private Joseph Clancey of the Pioneer Corps were on night guard duty outside Rudolf Hess's cellblock at Maindiff Court on September 2nd when Lieutenant Colonel Jeffries, the hospital Commandant, burst through the main door. Three persons followed closely behind him, a Scots Guards colonel in uniform, a bowler-hatted civilian and a strange-looking man in a black overcoat and a black felt hat and wearing dark glasses. They were immediately labelled "The Jock Colonel", "The Man from the Ministry" and "The Man in Black," by the Pioneer guards. Corporal Chalky unlocked Hess's cell to allow the 'visitors' access into the prisoner's living quarter and the Commandant was ordered to withdraw and to wait in the corridor with the Pioneers.

Not expecting visitors Hess was sitting on his bed in a bulky dark blue dressing gown. He sprang to his feet with a bewildered look on his face. He immediately recognised James but the 'stranger in black' looked menacing

"Wer ist der Man?" he demanded. Before James could reply Prost sprang to attention, removed his black hat and dark glasses, and formally saluted Hess.

"Herr Ernst Prost, Mein Führer."

Seemingly still uncertain about the whole situation Hess continued staring intently at Prost with his penetrating gaze. Prost now produced the replica Party medal he received from Hess in person in 1937. Satisfied that Prost was the 'real McCoy' Hess visibly relaxed and, for a full minute, they stared at each other in silence, the Nazi prisoner wondering if there was a catch in the late night visit and Prost mesmerized and overcome with emotion to be facing his former master. Hess eased himself backwards on to the edge of his bed while Ernst Prost remained standing stiffly to attention.

"Where were you taken prisoner, *Herr* Prost?" Hess asked.

"I was in Berlin until January. The Russians were advancing rapidly and I escaped north to Hamburg. I was arrested to save me from the Russians. I was pleased when the Colonel," and inclining his head towards James, "told me you had asked to see me, *Mein Führer*."

This made sense to Hess who was still doubtful about Ernst Prost's motives and his face lit up and softened.

"I am pleased you are safe Herr Prost," and, turning to face the two MI6 officers seated at the back of the bedroom, he asked.

"What is the purpose of Prost's visit? It cannot be for old times' sake."

Barlow moved forwards to stand next to Prost.

"*Herr* Prost wishes to be of assistance to you, *Herr Reichsminister*. He came here of his own free will and he has your interest at heart."

Hess looked stunned and arrogantly announced.

"I need no assistance. I am not ashamed of what I did for my Party and my Führer," and, with that, he stood on his feet and glared menacingly at the others. Barlow advanced towards Hess and, staring back into his green, malevolent eyes, he posed a rhetorical question.

"*Herr* Hess! You are aware you stand every chance of being executed after your trial? The Russians will insist on it. Our Government agree you have served your time and should now be released a free man. *Herr* Ernst Prost has volunteered to appear in your place at the Tribunal. Will you cooperate with us? I need your decision tonight."

"Will *Herr* Prost hang for me?" Hess spat out through

clenched teeth.

"After sentencing, *Herr* Prost will reveal his true identity and the Tribunal will have no choice but to release him. By that time you will be safely settled in a hideout. You will, of course, have to assume *Herr* Prost's name and lifestyle for the rest of your life. Do you agree with our plans for your future?"

Rudolf Hess was lost in deep concentration for half a minute during which time he had fleeting visions of leading Germany's revival from a position in exile. His dreams vanished into thin air as he faced the reality of his situation and he replied, "My wish to be buried next to the greatest German that ever lived has been denied and I will not be able to help my Fatherland's recovery from the war. If you assure me *Herr* Prost will not suffer on my behalf then I will agree to your proposed plan of action."

Barlow issued a sigh of relief, *"Danke Herr Reichsminister.* Arrangements will be made shortly."

At exactly midnight on that September 2nd, the three visitors to Hess's quarters took their leave. The Pioneer guards had been engaged in speculation about the identity of the 'stranger in black'. They came to a conclusion that he was either a British, or German, spy but they were unable to suggest an explanation for his visit to the quarters of the "Kaiser of Abergavenny" at such a late hour. Sulking because he had been excluded from the meeting in Hess's quarters, Colonel Jeffries might have had an answer to their quandary but he refused to involve himself in speculation about the identity of The Man in Black.

Barlow's work at Maindiff Court was now complete and he returned to MI6 to make arrangements for Hess's paperwork and his evacuation to a safe hideout overseas. Surprisingly Hess had shown no interest in his destination, or place of exile, if a 'switch' took place. He seemed more concerned about Prost's future at the impending Tribunal. Based at Gliffaes Manor Lieutenant Colonel James Sutherland was left in charge of the impostor and had the sole responsibility for arranging the 'switch'. The date for Rudolf Hess's transfer to Nuremberg was now known to MI6 and James had thirty-six days to perfect his plan of action.

In 1945 Gliffaes was in constant use as an Officers' Transit Mess for army units training in the locality. A staff bungalow at the rear of the hotel offered privacy and seclusion for James and Ernst Prost and they were completely segregated from the main Mess. Prost was prohibited from attempting to contact Mess members and was ordered to wear a peaked cap and dark glasses at all times out-of-doors. Though he spoke fluent German James insisted on improving Prost's English vocabulary and, in time, a comfortable working relationship was established between the German impostor, the Scots Guards Colonel and MI6 agents.

Throughout September 1945 James Sutherland made regular trips to visit Hess at Maindiff Court and, on a dozen occasions, arranged to take the "Kaiser of Abergavenny" to Gliffaes for a tea break. Accompanied by an armed guard, and a RASC driver, they motored to Gliffaes for an exchange of information session with Ernst Prost. Rudolf Hess's contribution at these meetings depended critically on his state of mind. At some sessions he was monosyllabic and kept his distance from Prost, adopting a supercilious attitude and treating his potential stand-in as a worthless subordinate. At other times he was in a talkative frame of mind and provided Prost with valuable information about his reign as Deputy Führer and his dealings with German and foreign diplomats he had encountered in the

1930s. One of his first revelations was to alert Prost that his 'Uncle Karl's' first wife died in 1891 and was buried in a churchyard near Cardiff. Hess considered it important Prost should be aware of the existence of 'Uncle Karl' and of the burial place of his first wife at Michaelstone-y-Fedw not more than thirty miles away from where they were sitting.

During a few tea parties at Gliffaes Rudolf Hess was in a super-manic mood and genuinely anxious to be of assistance to Prost in his planned deception. He described in detail the different treatment he received at Mytchett Place and Maindiff Court. For fourteen months at Camp Z he was under "close arrest" and guarded by Scots guardsmen commanded by Captain Sutherland. Later, in February 1942, the Scots Guards were replaced by Pioneers and they moved across to Maindiff with Hess in July. The routine at Mytchett was strictly controlled – no razors and sharp instruments and cutlery; only censored week-old newspapers; no radio bulletins and exercise in the paddock restricted to one hour each morning and evening. Hess had to sleep with a bright light shining in his bedroom all night and any sketches and diary entries were confiscated at the end of each day, scrutinized and presumably destroyed. He had frequent interrogations by Government officials and he dealt with their questioning by pleading loss of memory. Numerous psychiatrists examined him at Camp Z and a Jewish doctor, Major Dicks, was outwardly unsympathetic. Hess admitted his fourteen months at Mytchett Place were mentally extremely stressful and drove him to attempt suicide in June 1941. He recognised he had become depressed at camp Z and he counteracted the stress and perpetual pressure and questioning by developing prolonged bouts of amnesia which he had learnt to exhibit at will.

In his detention quarters at Maindiff Court Hess described fewer restrictions, receiving a daily newssheet, listening to the radio, perusing books from the hospital library and keeping an uncensored diary and sketchbooks. He was allowed to receive a letter from Germany, and write a reply home, every month. He was, however, still restricted to using a safety razor for shaving and he ate his meals with blunt cutlery. Once a week Hess was physically examined by Dr Griffiths, the Hospital Superintendent, who checked his weight and recorded his blood pressure. Maindiff's resident psychiatrist, Major Ellis Jones, regularly interviewed Hess but neither he, nor any other mental specialist, could fathom the cause of his bouts of amnesia. On quite a number of occasions at the tea party at Gliffaes Hess gloated over his ability to feign this memory loss and fool the interrogators and medical staff.

According to Hess the great advantage of incarceration at Maindiff was extra freedom to get out in the open air. The hospital authorities allowed him to spend afternoons sketching at White Castle and on the banks of the river Usk. He was taken for walks on the Skirrid Mountains and the Sugar Loaf and for a glass of unpalatable, tepid ale at the Walnut Tree pub. He had had occasional lunches at the White House, the Hospital Commandant's quarters combined with an Officers' Mess, near a canal on the outskirts of Abergavenny. As an extra bonus, and in suitable conditions, Hess used the exercise compound outside his cellblock at any time in daylight hours provided he was accompanied by a Pioneer guard. He failed to mention, however, that he made an abortive suicide attempt, as recently as February 1945, by stabbing himself twice in the chest with a bread knife. When challenged by James about the incident, Hess's face went blank and, convincingly, he stated he could not recall doing such a thing and this despite the evidence of two recent one-inch scars on his chest wall. James Sutherland had a gut feeling Ernst Prost was sympathetic to Hess's anti-Jewish tirades. He stressed on Prost to exhibit Hess's paranoid symptoms at the impending trial and, if all else failed and he was in difficulties, his sure defensive shield was amnesia.

A list of indicted Nazi war criminals was common knowledge in Government circles by November 1944. James Sutherland insisted Prost would need to know intimate details about his co-conspirators in Dock and the best source of information would be Rudolf Hess. He sought permission from MI6 to reveal the list to Hess and he did so at Gliffaes in the second week of September. Four indicted Nazis on the original list – Hitler, Göebbels, Himmler and Martin Bormann, were presumed dead and automatically excluded. At the commencement of the Tribunal they were tried in their absence, found guilty on all charges, and condemned to death in absentia. The remaining twenty-three were expected to appear in court at Nuremberg in the first and second weeks in October 1945.

At one Gliffaes tea break James, slowly and deliberately, read out the names of Nazis indictees scheduled to appear at the Tribunal. Rudolf Hess winced as some of the individuals were mentioned. Meanwhile Prost looked on, scrutinising Rudolf's face and mentally recording his reactions. Rudolf Hess was slow to respond and his responses were frequently ambivalent. At first he was deeply concerned about the possible fate of his Nazi compatriots but, eventually, information about the Party and his international contacts came gushing forth in a steady torrent. His insight and knowledge about past events in the thirties made a mockery of his claim to be unable to remember what happened in Germany at that time.

Hess was fully aware of the actions of his Nazi colleagues who had perpetrated many heinous crimes on behalf of Adolf Hitler and was acquainted with all the persons named on James Sutherland's 'black list', but it soon became evident his connection with most of them was purely on a casual basis. He detested Wehrmacht generals Jodl and Keitel and only tolerated the naval admirals Raeder and Döenitz. The arrogant Prussian generals annoyed him with their superior, aristocratic attitudes and they treated Hess like an inexperienced novice in his input into the Nazi war machine. He then described his closer contacts with Air *Reichsmarschal* Hermann Göering and envisaged he would be a major problem if he suspected Ernst Prost to be an impostor.

"I first met Göering in 1922. We were both students at Munich University. He was a war hero and a fighter ace in Richtofen's Flying Circus. Göering did not fit in with the University students and his clique was made up of retired officers, diplomats and wealthy businessmen. He occasionally attended our meetings and, in the early days, poked fun at *Mein Führer*. Marching by the side of General Ludendorf he did take part in the Beer Hall Putsch in 1923. He suffered a gunshot wound in the leg. He then married and disappeared to Sweden. After his wife died in 1926 he returned to Germany and rejoined our Party. He was ambitious to become leader from the very beginning. Göering was jealous of my position as the Führer's deputy and did not try to hide his contempt at my closeness to the Führer. At the outbreak of the war he pushed himself closer to *Mein Führer* but he could never displace me as the Führer's right-hand man. Göering is a dangerous, scheming man. He will definitely be inquisitive and will try to get *Herr* Prost involved in his schemes. He will be the one man most likely to question whether *Herr* Prost might be a duplicate for me."

James saw his opportunity to interrogate Hess and asked, "Were you displaced as Deputy Führer by the *Air Reichsmarschal*?" Eyes blazing in anger, Hess jumped to his feet.

"No! No! After the fall of France we both volunteered to come across to England to seek peace. *Mein Führer* agreed I should go."

"Did Göering know about your flight beforehand?" James asked. Thoroughly rattled, Hess spat out a reply.

"I do not believe that Hermann knew and, what is more, I do not care if he did know. We never were on friendly terms and, by 1940, Göering was intent on displacing *Mein Führer*."

With that he shut up like a clam and the information session came to an abrupt impasse. It took a good hour for Hess to overcome his violent outburst and he then resorted to generalities and dealt with each indictee individually. He stated he had met with all the men on the list during his time as Deputy Führer. The casual meetings were not a basis for closer relationships and he did not think people like Kaltenbrunner, Rosenberg, Frick, Frank, Streicher, von Neurath, von Papen, von Schirach and Seys-Inquart would cause concern if Prost was to meet them face-to-face. Hess had reservations about a few of his former colleagues.

"There are four men on the list who may question your identity, *Herr* Prost. I have spoken about Hermann Göering. The other three are von Ribbentrop, Albert Speer and Walter Funk." James asked politely if Hess felt up to talking about his three close Nazi colleagues. Hess replied, "Yes. I wish to be of assistance to *Herr* Prost. He may be sacrificing his liberty on my behalf. I will speak now. *Herr* Prost must be careful in dealing with Joachim von Ribbentrop. He came to the Party leadership from nowhere in 1933 and worked his way up the ladder to become German Ambassador in London in 1935. He cultivated a close relationship with your King Edward VIII and his consort. His affairs with wives of British nobility, and Mrs Wallace Simpson, led to his premature return to Germany shortly after King Edward's coronation in January 1936. When the Duke and Duchess of Windsor visited the Führer's Berghof in October 1937, von Ribbentrop was despatched out of the way to visit Mussolini in Italy and to avoid embarrassment for Hitler's royal guests. In 1936 Von Ribbentrop took over the German Foreign Ministry from Franz von Papen and, together, we organised 1938's Austrian Anschluss -- but he took all the credit. You will find von Ribbentrop charming and polite but beware of him. He is sly and underhanded and will go to any lengths to save his own skin. I was not an intimate colleague of either Göering or von Ribbentrop but, for the sake of Party solidarity, I toed the line."

Rudolf Hess paused and asked for a glass of milk. Ernst Prost sat attentively throughout this monologue, speechless, mesmerised and besotted by the fact he was in the presence of his fallen idol. After a few minutes silence there was more to come from Hess.

"Between 1933 and 1939 I organised the annual Nuremberg Party Rallies. In 1934 Albert Speer arrived on the scene to assist me and immediately became the Führer's favourite, mainly because of his architectural background. Together, the Führer and Speer planned to rebuild Berlin's state buildings in the Gothic style to become a grandiose capital city. Very soon Speer was constantly present at the Führer's side, at state functions and at the Berghof in Obersalzburg. He was not politically ambitious and was content to stay in the background. His architectural training and attention to detail helped to make the Party rallies spectacular events worthy of worldwide acclamation. We worked amicably together and spent many hours in each other's company. Always respectful of my rank and position Speer was a faithful and dependable colleague and I am sad to hear he will stand trial and probably lose his life purely for believing in, and planning for, the future of the Third Reich. Speer will be certain to befriend you, *Herr* Prost. If he asks tricky questions about our time together in Munich and Nuremberg you should pretend to be forgetful. Albert Speer will understand your difficulties."

Saddened by thoughts of the potential loss of so many Party loyalists, Hess stopped speaking again for a lengthy pause. Gathering his thoughts together for one final effort he spoke up for the last time.

"There is another Party member you will meet at the trial who probably will make friends with you. President of the Reichsbank, and Minister for Economics, Walter Funk had total control over the Party's finances and was invaluable to my Department as a source of revenue for my projects. He is quiet and self-effacing and, like myself, a believer in natural remedies for healthy living. Walter Funk knows me well and he was the last Party member I spoke to on the telephone before I took off to fly to England. Our conversation was entirely about Party funding. Funk will be certain to approach you *Herr* Prost. I doubt if he will have any queries about your identity."

Seemingly exhausted and complaining of stomach cramps, Hess asked for another glass of milk or a cup of herbal tea. The information session had reached its conclusion with the main speaker empty and drained. Hess was silent throughout the car journey back to Maindiff Court Hospital.

Throughout his captivity in Britain Hess's attitude towards members of the Nazi Party had always been evasive and was never a subject for discussion. Under interrogation, more often than not, he relapsed into a state of amnesia as a defensive shield. At the Gliffaes tea break on that September afternoon James Sutherland was impressed by Hess's revelations and candid feelings about his one-time Nazi colleagues. It appeared Rudolph was experiencing relief from bottled-up emotions he had harboured about Party members throughout his years in captivity on British soil. It may also indicate that Hess's amnesia was a cleverly concocted smokescreen devised to fool his interrogators and medical specialists. James Sutherland accepted Hess's information as a definite indication of his wholehearted commitment to the 'switch' and his readiness to assume the personality and lifestyle of Ernst Prost. And Prost had already made it clear that, with his physical similarity to Rudolf Hess and his stage-acting ability, he was more than prepared to stand in the witness box for the one-time Deputy Führer. The stage was set for a 'switch' and, on the last day in September, James Sutherland was instructed, to set the wheels in motion for an exchange at Maindiff Court on the 9th of October 1945.

THE "MAINDIFF SWITCH"

9TH OCTOBER 1945

Rudolf Hess's transfer from Maindiff court to face trial at Nuremberg was scheduled to take place in the early hours of the 10th of October 1945. MI6 agent Barlow booked in at the Angel Hotel in Abergavenny on the 7th of October and brought with him moth-eaten photographs and false identity papers, in the name of Ernst Prost, for Hess to display should the 'switch' prove to be successful. The MI6 agent and Maindiff's senior psychiatrist, Major Ellis Jones, had been delegated to accompany Hess, or as it transpired his impostor, on the flight to Nuremberg. An armed Military Police sergeant and a lance corporal kept guard over the "Kaiser of Abergavenny" on his return flight to his homeland.

Corporal Chalky White and Private Joey were on guard duty outside Hess's detention quarters on the night of the 9th of October and took over from their Pioneer Corps buddies at 8.00pm. Hess had been prepared for bed by day staff before they came on duty and, as required by regulations, the hospital Commandant and an RAMC orderly looked in on the prisoner at 10.00pm. They reported Hess was reading in bed and settling down for the night. All was then silent and peaceful and the Corporal and Private Joey took it in turns to wander outside into the courtyard for a quick smoke, or to brew a pot of tea on a portable Calor-gas stove in the kitchen. For the Pioneer guards it was a normal duty night until 11.10pm when motorcar headlights were seen approaching from the courtyard and loud voices were heard outside the hospital's main entrance. Within a minute the Camp Commandant, Lieutenant Colonel John Jeffries, came striding down the corridor closely followed by Lieutenant Colonel Sutherland and the man dressed from head to toe in black and wearing dark glasses, both of whom the Pioneers recognised from their previous visit to the prisoner's quarters. Colonel Jeffries demanded two sets of keys and unlocked both doors, which allowed Sutherland and the "Man in Black" entry into Rudolf Hess's cellblock. Jeffries then retired to sit at the Pioneers' desk in the corridor. Probing questions from Corporal Chalky failed to elicit any information as to the nature of this unexpected visit. Colonel Jeffries only confirmed he had received a phone call from H.Q. at 10.30pm to expect Colonel Sutherland and a civilian and to ensure their immediate access into Hess's quarters.

Lieutenant Colonel Sutherland and Ernst Prost were alone with Hess in his bedroom for half an hour. Known to be an insomniac, and a light sleeper, Rudolf Hess was quickly wide-awake when Sutherland walked up to his bedside. For many days Hess had nursed a feeling that his transfer to Germany to stand trial was fast approaching, but the sudden appearance of the Scots Guards Colonel and *Herr* Prost at a late hour came as a complete surprise. With questioning, suspicious eyes he asked James, "Is it time for me to leave, *Herr* Colonel?"

"Yes, *Herr Reichsminister*. When we depart from here you will be known as *Herr* Prost."

Hess gave a sigh of relief as if a heavy burden had been taken off his shoulders. Prost now undressed down to his underpants and Hess put on the very clothes, including underwear, worn by Prost when he was brought across from Hamburg to Britain. Sutherland then passed on Ernst Prost's fake documents to Hess together with a generous wad of American dollar bills and, after he had dressed in Prost's black coat, black hat and dark glasses, he became "The Man in Black." In the meantime Prost had donned Hess's pyjamas and dark blue hospital dressing gown and stood aside with a look of awe, mixed with admiration, on his face. As they were about to leave the prisoner's quarters Hess turned to face his stand-in.

"The time has come, *Herr* Prost. It is not too late to change your mind. Are you still prepared to take my place?"

Draped in Hess's bulky, dark-blue dressing gown Prost stood to attention and replied, "I am honoured to stand in for you, *mein* Deputy Führer."

Pleased with Prost's reference to his previous status Hess responded.

"In that case I wish you luck, *Herr* Prost," and he strode out of the bedroom which had been his living quarters for over three-and-a-half years.

The Pioneer guards and the Camp Commandant sat together in silence at the sentry desk in the corridor. Colonel Jeffries was in a foul mood, evidently annoyed he had not been invited into Hess's cell by James Sutherland. Their silent vigil was rudely interrupted by a loud banging on Hess's door. Colonel Jeffries unlocked the safety catches to allow Lieutenant Colonel Sutherland and the "Man in Black" to emerge into the corridor. The Pioneer guards stood to attention as the visitors swept past their sentry post and Corporal Chalky swore he heard the 'civilian in black' mouthing the words *'Danke Mein Soldats'* as he passed the desk. The hospital Commandant ushered his visitors out through the main entrance and, a few minutes later, the roar of a revving engine heralded departure of their car. The Commandant returned to supervise locking the prison doors securely and then he left the building. Little did he realise the man in detention under his care was no longer Rudolf Hess, the "Kaiser of Abergavenny", but a stand-up comedian and part-time actor called Ernst Prost.

As soon as Colonel Jeffries had departed Private Joey looked across the desk at his companion on sentry duty. "What the 'ell was all that about, Corp?" Corporal Chalky White seemed bemused. "I 'aven't a clue, Joey," and, pointing at Hess's cell, he continued, "There's something big goin' on with 'im inside. We'll soon find out. Go and brew-up Joey and make it stronger this time. Your last brew was like cat's piss!" With a chuckle Joey retorted "Okay Corp. Keep your 'air on."

By midnight on the 9th of October, peace and serenity reigned once more at the sentry point guarding Hess's cellblock and the two Pioneers took it in turn to rest while his companion kept watch in the corridor. The sentries' tranquil vigilance was, however, interrupted for a second time on their watch at around 3.45am on the 10th of October. Daybreak was still two hours away and there was a distinct chill in the autumnal breeze. Joey was outside in the courtyard smoking a cigarette when a vehicle, with headlights blazing, came off the road and pulled up for a minute outside the hospital's main gate. It then began ascending the long driveway to the hospital main entrance. At this point Joey ground his fag into the gravel and, picking up his rifle, hastily withdrew inside. Corporal Chalky White sat dozing at the sentry desk. Private Joey bellowed, "Wakey, wakey, Corp! There's another car on the way up 'ere. It'll be with us in a minute!" Corporal White woke with a start and frenziedly tidied-up the desk and adjusted his crumpled battledress. Picking up his Lee-Enfield rifle he took up a position in front of the desk and ordered Joey to stand to attention at the entrance to Hess's cellblock.

The first person to come down the corridor was an armed Redcap, a British Military Police sergeant, closely followed by Colonel Jeffries who demanded the keys to Hess's quarters for the second time that night. Next came two persons, one in the uniform of a Medical Corps Major and the other, a bowler-hatted civilian. The Major was Maindiff Hospital's chief psychiatrist, Dr Ellis Jones, accompanied by a civilian MI6 agent, Charles Barlow, referred to by the Pioneer guards as 'the Man from the Ministry.' On this occasion Jeffries was allowed into the prisoner's cell with the R.A.M.C. major and the MI6 agent. The Redcap sergeant sat down with the Pioneers and readily accepted a quick brew-up. He was quite chatty and let it slip that "'e was 'ere to pick-up 'im inside and take 'im to Germany to face the music."

Rudolf Hess's impostor, *Herr* Ernst Prost, had managed a couple of hours sleep but he was fully awake when the unannounced visitors arrived in his bedroom. Colonel Jeffries ordered 'Hess' to shave and brush-up and to don Hess's favourite pale-blue Luftwaffe tunic and trousers. Fur-lined boots, a leather flying jacket and a blue, peaked cap completed his ensemble. He was not allowed to take any personal objects, or memorabilia, with him from Maindiff Court. The uniform fitted Prost like a glove and outwardly, to all intents and purposes, he was Rudolf Hess. Of the seven persons present at Hess's detention cell in Maindiff Court at around 4:00 am on the 10th of October 1945 only two were aware of the 'switch' – *Herr* Ernst Prost himself and Charles Barlow of MI6.

After half an hour in Hess's quarters the visiting party emerged and filed past Chalky White's guard post. The two Pioneers stood rigidly at attention and watched their prize prisoner being ushered down the corridor and into a military vehicle in the courtyard. When the Humber was driven away Corporal Chalky spoke to Joey.

"That's the last we'll see of 'im. 'E weren't a bad lot for a Nazi, a bit bonkers but we got on with 'im alright, didn't we Joey?"

"Yes we did Corp. Fancy another brew-up?"

"I wouldn't say no, Joey," Corporal White replied.

Ten minutes later Colonel Jeffries returned and locked up Hess's empty prison quarters. Handing over the keys to Corporal White he ordered the Pioneers not to discuss what happened that night with anyone for at least 24 hours and at hand-over of the keys to the day sentries at 8:00am. They were not to enter the events of that night in the duty report adding, "No one, I repeat no one, is to be allowed entry into the prisoner's quarters until I get around to it tomorrow morning. Is that clear, Corporal?"

"Yes, Sir," the Pioneer guards answered in unison, but the last order was like a red rag to a bull. As soon as the Hospital Commandant left the detention block they burst into Hess's cell searching for souvenirs. Their foray was only partially successful. There were masses of paper sheets and notebooks, hand-written in German, and a virtual library of books, but nothing of tangible value as souvenirs for the Pioneers. They did pocket a few of Hess's pencil sketches and water colours of the rural areas surrounding Maindiff Court and Joey snatched a Felinfoel flagon label allegedly signed by Rudolf Hess at the Walnut Tree Inn. Corporal Chalky White's prize acquisition was a replica, bronze medallion, dated 1921, of Rudolf Hess's Party membership number 16. (The signed flagon label has survived the ravages of time and is on display at a museum in

Abergavenny's town centre. The sketches and the bronze membership medallion have been lost forever).

The 'switch' at Maindiff Court hospital occurred at around 11:00pm on October 9th 1945. Assuming the identity of Ernst Prost, Hess was transported to an army barracks at Cardiff in preparation for his eventual escape into exile in South America. Within five hours of the 'real' Hess's departure from Maindiff Court another staff car transported Ernst Prost from Abergavenny to an airfield at Madley, outside Hereford. An armed Military Police sergeant sat next to the R.A.S.C. driver and Prost was wedged in the back seat between Major Ellis Jones and Charles Barlow of MI6. Departure of the passenger-carrying Dakota was delayed for four hours and the plane eventually took off from Madley at 9.30am on the 10th of October. The Dakota refuelled in Brussels and landed in Nuremberg at 4.00pm. The party was transported to the Palace of Justice where the decoy Hess was placed in cell 125. Having handed their prisoner into the custody of the U.S Military Police, referred to as 'snowdrops' due to their practice of wearing white helmets, belts and gaiters, the British party flew home on the same day.

Lieutenant Colonel James Sutherland was particularly pleased with himself. He had been a major player in the scam to replace the "Kaiser of Abergavenny" with an impostor, hopefully capable of appearing on Hess's behalf at the Nuremberg War Crimes Tribunal. Sutherland's contribution led to one of the major unsolved mysteries of World War II. What eventually happened to the 'real' Rudolf Hess remains an enigma to this very day. It is certain that an enormous amount of speculation and literature exists, and the general public's thirst for knowledge prevails, about the mystery surrounding the identity of Prisoner No.7 at Spandau. The mode of his death be he the 'real' Rudolf Hess or a *doppelgänger* introduced to replace him by a 'switch' at Maindiff Court Hospital in Abergavenny, is still an unsolved mystery.

RUDOLF HESS IN EXILE

10TH OCTOBER 1945 – 30TH JANUARY 1946

The maindiff 'switch' took place at around 11:00pm on the 9th of october 1945. Rudolf hess, alias ernst prost, and lieutenant colonel james sutherland were conveyed in a Humber staff car to Maindee Barracks in the centre of Cardiff. The journey took about an hour and they arrived at their destination just after midnight. Hess was placed in a detention cell in the guardhouse and remained under maximum security for two days while James Sutherland spent his time at Cardiff Docks, finalising arrangements for 'Herr Prost's' transfer out of Britain to a safe haven in South America. Packed with naval shipping during the war Cardiff docks were rapidly reconverting to peacetime commercial trade. A vessel pinpointed by MI6 suited Sutherland's purpose down to the ground. The *Punta del Esté*, a 12,000 tonne cargo ship laden with coal and iron ore, was due to sail to Montevideo in Uruguay on the 14th of October. In the name of Ernst Prost, and with a generous dollar backhander for the Captain, Rudolf Hess was signed on as a passenger-cum-deckhand for a one-way transatlantic crossing to Buenos Aires on the *Punta del Esté*.

Towards the end of 1944, and throughout 1945 and 1946, Brazil, Argentina and Uruguay became 'safe havens' on South America's Atlantic seaboard for Nazi war criminals fleeing from Europe. With its 3,800 mile Atlantic coastline Brazil would be their main target but she declared war on the Axis powers in August 1942 following the sinking of two Brazilian cargo vessels by Nazi U-Boats. As a consequence Brazil virtually became a 'no-go' destination for escaping German nationals. When the Nazi war machine was in full swing, and military conquests came on a regular basis, Argentina served as a refuelling base for German U-boats and cargo vessels. By January 1944 the balance of power in World War II had swung in favour of the Allies and the Argentinians were reluctantly persuaded to break off relations with Germany. Meanwhile Uruguay remained neutral throughout the entire conflict and Germany, Japan, Great Britain and the USA had fully-staffed embassies at Montevideo. Each and every country had a full quota of embassy espionage and counter-espionage agents. Their clandestine operations were supported by cadres of corrupt Uruguayan 'officials' recruited by the agents. It took little time for secret information from one embassy to become common knowledge at other diplomatic agencies. The focal entry points for illegal immigrants were centred around the estuary of the River Plate, Montevideo in Uruguay to the north and, 75 miles across the river to the south, La Plata and Buenos Aires in Argentina. The main Nazi escape route in Europe was via Switzerland to northern Italian ports, thence to embark on cargo ships bound for South America. Consequently an expanding hoard of Nazi 'exiles,' mainly SS Officers who feared they would be condemned to death if they remained in Germany, congregated around the estuary of the River Plate in 1945 and 1946.

The British embassy maintained a vigilant group of officials at Montevideo and, via diplomatic channels, MI6 had forewarned them to expect the arrival of an illegal immigrant in the name of Ernst Prost on a cargo vessel, the *Punta del Esté*, any time between the 23rd and 27th of October. They were ordered to keep Prost under surveillance and arrange accommodation for him in the countryside outside Montevideo. He was to be provided with housekeepers and a monthly stipend and kept clear from undesirable German nationals who were known to be in exile and actively operating in Uruguay. If 'Prost' was questioned about his escape from Germany a foolproof story had been concocted for him. He was instructed to say he found a stash of American dollars in a derelict, bombed-out house in Prinz-Alberz Plaz, just off the Reeperbahn, in Hamburg. With the money he went to the bomb-scarred docks and bought his passage as a deckhand on a cargo vessel. The *Punta del Esté* was transporting iron ore from Göthenberg in Sweden and called in Cardiff in South Wales to take aboard a load of coal and provisions. The cargo vessel sailed from Cardiff on its transatlantic crossing on the 14th of October 1945.

The Uruguayan cargo vessel, with Rudolf Hess aboard, developed engine trouble 200 miles out of Montevideo and eventually limped into its parent harbour at Punta del Esté on the 24th October. The unexpected arrival of a suspect refugee by sea triggered off a hive of activity at foreign embassies in Montevideo. The British embassy had been alerted of a change in the ship's schedule and two of their agents were at the dockside at Punta del Esté to supervise '*Herr* Prost's' transit through customs and immigration, which literally meant bribing the Uruguayan port authorities. Port officials lost no time in informing German and Japanese embassies in Montevideo of the arrival of a German national by the name of Ernst Prost and, for this information, they were well compensated by the Committee for Expatriate Nazis in Montevideo. 'Prost' was regarded as a minor Party member and one ex-SS officer in the group had witnessed his stage performance as a 'Hess' look-alike at Potsdam a few weeks before he was gaoled, and banned from acting, in January 1944. Two questions went unanswered – why 'Prost' had disembarked in Punta del Esté and not Montevideo where 'friendly,' paid Uruguayans would have monitored him on landing and, secondly, why he was met at Punta del Esté dockside by British secret agents? This stimulated interest from the fledgling Nazi committee and they made a decision to look into the affairs of 'Herr Ernst Prost' in due course.

By October 1945 there were already a group of around 40 ardent, dyed-in-the-wool Nazi defectors in Montevideo and its environs and a similar number based 95 miles across the River Plate at Buenos Aires. British embassy officials were fully aware of these Nazi hard-liners and had made careful plans to whisk 'Herr Prost' away to a safe-house in the hinterland, half way along the 70-mile stretch of main road between Punta del Este and Montevideo. The secluded farmhouse was surrounded by orchards and approached along a beaten track branching off a secondary road leading northwards to the township of Migues. The villa was fully furnished and staffed by trustworthy husband and wife caretakers and a locally-based, middle-aged, Spanish-speaking gardener called Fernando. He took care of the orchards and a large vegetable garden. A British embassy 'official' was permanently present at the villa and rotated weekly from his headquarters at Montevideo. Most of the embassy agents were generous and accompanied 'Herr Prost' on daily walks outside the villa and into the surrounding woodland. As armed guards their function was to prevent 'Prost' wandering off on his own and attempting to make contact with the fanatic Nazi exiles who had settled in the countryside around Montevideo. With this in mind the British

Embassy made a point of not installing a telephone at the villa.

Rudolf Hess settled down quickly in his newfound 'freedom.' The Uruguayan caretakers were courteous and efficient and took good care of all his needs, including his vegetarian diet and his dependency on herbal remedies. The gardener, Fernando, was friendly and chatty though his limited English and German vocabulary was a bar to lengthy conversations. Hess was able to select his own reading books and he was provided with writing and sketching materials. In the evenings he was allowed to listen to news broadcasts in German and English, which kept him up-to-date with the progress of his compatriots at the International Military Tribunal in Nuremberg. Hess's main cause for frustration was the presence of an embassy guard at the villa for 24 hours a day, which denied him complete freedom and reminded him of the interminable days of incarceration in wartime Britain.

During his time at Maindiff Court, weather permitting, Rudolf Hess had been a stickler for exercising every day. Uruguay's sub-tropical climate, and the larch wood forests surrounding the farmhouse, allowed ample opportunity to satisfy his passion for keeping fit and exercising in the open air. His diurnal two-mile walk from the villa usually started off with a brisk scamper through the fruit trees in the orchard and he occasionally stopped to have a few words with the gardener. Outside the fenced boundary of the orchard he strolled along the bank of a brook for two thousand yards and the narrow stream disappeared into a copse of spruce trees. The ground then started rising gently and the spruce gave way to a thick larch wood forest. Hess's favourite resting place was on a flat boulder beside a ten-foot waterfall about 400 yards inside the forest. He would sit on the boulder for at least half an hour, sketching, or reading a book. His exercise sessions were not conducted with complete freedom. As unobtrusively as possible an armed embassy guard walked fifty yards behind '*Herr* Prost'. The guard usually stopped short at a point where the brook meandered through the spruce bushes, on the assumption the German had nowhere to go and the ground rose steeply uphill at the waterfall in the forest. He also reckoned any unwanted visitors would have to approach '*Herr* Prost' along the bank of the meandering brook.

By Christmas 1945 Hess was getting restless. His lengthy years in captivity in Britain, between May 1941 and October 1945, were fresh in his memory and reports of suffering in his beloved Fatherland increased his eagerness to re-enter the political arena and to meet with like-minded Germans exiled in Montevideo. The Third Reich had collapsed and was now leaderless and the German people would need a new leader to guide them out of the abyss. Hess's private visions came to fruition sooner than he expected. One fine sunny morning, on the 28th of January 1946, Hess disappeared from his usual resting place at the waterfall in the larch-wood forest. He did not disappear without trace. He left behind on the boulder his white canvas satchel containing sketchpads, crayons and pencils and a moth-eaten copy of 'Three Men in a Boat.' An explanation of 'Ernst Prost's' mysterious disappearance was linked to the actions of the Argentinean gardener at the farmhouse. He also disappeared from the villa on the 28th January 1946 and disappeared to return to his homeland in Argentina.

Within a month of the war in Europe ending in May 1945, Nazi exiles in the vicinity of Montevideo had formed an ad-hoc junta of three ex-SS Officers to vet and check the authenticity of allegedly Nazi refugees arriving in Uruguay. Their leader was a self-styled Waffen SS Major who had been involved in ethnic cleansing operations in Poland and Russia. Major Müller and his junta colleagues were aware of 'Ernst Prost's' unexpected arrival at Punta del Esté and his subsequent disappearance into the Uruguayan hinterland. Regarded as a low-ranking Nazi they had not made extra efforts to ascertain 'Prost's' whereabouts until the gardener from the villa turned up at the German embassy two days before Christmas 1945. Fernando had been given leave during the Christmas break to visit his cousin's family in Montevideo. While he was in the city he passed on details about '*Herr* Ernst Prost's' daily routine at the farmhouse near Migues to German embassy officials. For this information he was paid sixty-five American dollars.

Acting on the gardener's information Major Müller dispatched two of his henchmen, to pick up '*Herr* Prost' and bring him to Montevideo for questioning. They were ordered to get into the larch-wood forest an hour before 'Prost' was expected to turn up at the waterfall. A man of habit, and dead on cue, 'Prost' arrived at 11:00am and settled down on the boulder to do some sketching. The escorting British embassy guard habitually retired to the edge of the spruce bushes and sat down on the riverbank to smoke a cigarette and relax in the warm sunshine. Out of the blue two men suddenly appeared walking down a meandering pathway in the larch trees. Startled, Hess dropped his sketching pad and sprang to his feet to meet the intruders. With a smile on his face, and in a quiet voice, one of the men spoke in cultured German.

"*Herr* Ernst Prost? We are from the German embassy in Montevideo."

Immediately on the defensive, Hess responded in German, "What do you want with me?"

The German spokesman replied, "We represent the Third Reich in Uruguay. We are defending the Nazi cause and want you to join us."

Flattered, Rudolf Hess was immediately interested and, as an ex-Colonel General in the SS, he suddenly visualised becoming the leader of the Nazi faction in Uruguay. Without hesitation he asked.

"How can I do that?"

"You must come with us today to meet our Gauleiter in Montevideo." Hess looked dubious at first but, after a minute's consideration, made up his mind to go along with the intruders. Putting on his leather, peaked cap and dark glasses and placing his sketching pad and white, canvas satchel on the boulder, he squared his shoulders and announced.

"I am ready. I will follow you."

The German embassy agents and Rudolf Hess ploughed their way upwards through the thick forest undergrowth to a scrub-covered plateau. Walking westwards for three miles they descended to ground level and were only 200 yards away from the main road to Montevideo. In a converted Jeep, a driver was waiting at the roadside and, an hour after 'Prost' was picked up at the waterfall in the forest, they were on their way to Montevideo.

Luxuriating at the riverbank in the warm sun, and smoking a cheroot, the embassy guard became restless when he realised 'Prost' had overstayed his rest period at the waterfall by 20 minutes. He entered the larch-wood forest and found 'Prost's' satchel on the boulder and a few of his sketches strewn on the ground. He immediately assumed the German had gone further into the wood to relieve himself. Shouting 'Prost's' name the guard explored among the nearest larch trees but there were no signs of the missing German. He hurried back to the villa. The caretakers denied seeing '*Herr* Prost' after he left the villa for his ritual walk at around 10:30am. They joined forces with the guard for a further search in the larch-wood and one leaf of 'Prost's' sketching pad was discovered on a tangled pathway in the forest's depths. By now, thoroughly concerned, the guard decided to raise the alarm. The nearest telephone booth was nine miles away on the forecourt of a roadside taverna and by the time the embassy guard got through to his headquarters in Montevideo it was nearly two o'clock in the afternoon. By that time Rudolf Hess was preparing to board a ferry boat due to make its daily crossing to La Plata and Buenos Aires in Argentina.

The meeting place of exiled Nazi fanatics in Montevideo was in a disused warehouse in the docks area of the city and Hess, and the two Nazi henchmen, reached their destination at around 2:00pm. In the dim light inside the warehouse a four-man reception committee headed by *Herr* Müller, the self-appointed Gauleiter in Montevideo, sat behind a trestle table. A thickset, bald-headed, brute of a man, sporting a Prussian military moustache, Müller began in an aggressive manner by asking a rhetorical question.

"You are Ernst Prost?" and then he ordered Hess to remove his cap and dark glasses. Hess obliged and glared at Müller with his penetrating, steely stare. The committee exchanged glances of disbelief and were obviously curious, and somewhat uncomfortable, at Prost's likeness in appearance to Adolf Hitler's one-time Deputy Führer. Hess took an immediate dislike to 'Major' Müller and, sensing the committee's discomfiture, he decided to go on the attack.

"And who are you?"

Major Müller's attitude stiffened. "I am Major Müller of the Waffen SS. And you, what did you do in the war?" The belligerent Major's attitude riled Hess further and his hackles rose. In a fit of uncontrollable anger he exploded.

"I am Standarte SS Colonel General Rudolf Hess, Adolf Hitler's Deputy Führer."

Müller looked at him scornfully.

"How can we believe you, *Herr* Prost? British agents met you in Punta del Esté. The traitor Hess is on trial in Nuremberg." Hess was furious and went on a counter-attack.

"Do you have a senior officer? I will only explain everything to him."

Müller was now out of his depth. He did not for a minute believe 'Prost's' improbable story and the arrogance 'Prost' displayed annoyed him and, yet, Müller did not wish to put a foot wrong to antagonise his superiors in Buenos Aires. After all was said and done he was only a minor cog in the Nazi exiles' organisation in South America. He quickly decided to refer the suspect to higher authority.

"Our commander in Buenos Aires is a Wehrmacht Major General. You will be taken to him today." Standing upright Rudolf Hess stared belligerently at Müller and his cronies and offered a Nazi salute.

"I order you to do that, *Herr* Mayor."

Müller did not return the salute. Furious at 'Prost's' obvious snub to his authority he lost control and, pointing towards the exit, he bellowed.

"Take him out of my sight. Put him on this afternoon's ferryboat to Buenos Aires. They'll deal with him there."

There were two ferryboat sailings each day from Montevideo, across the River Plate estuary, to La Plata and

Buenos Aires in Argentina. Regarded as an internal service, customs and immigration were lax and relatively free access between the two countries was accepted. Accompanied by two henchmen from the Nazi Junta in Montevideo, Rudolf Hess boarded the afternoon ferryboat from the commercial dock at 4.00pm on 28th January 1946 and this was the last positive sighting of the one-time Deputy Führer. What happened to him on his voyage across the River Plate, or on disembarkation at either La Plata or Buenos Aires, remains a mystery but one thing is certain- Ernst Prost's alias, Rudolf Hess, was never seen again in public.

Speculation about Hess's eventual fate in South America may be only open to debatable conjecture. One theory suggests the Commander of the Nazi faction in Montevideo changed his mind and ordered his henchmen to execute Hess on the ferryboat and dispose of his body overboard under cover of darkness. No records of a suspect resembling Rudolf Hess disembarking at either La Plata, or Buenos Aires, exists and, if this speculation is correct, Rudolf Hess's final resting place is in the depths of the turbid waters of the River Plate. The second theory allows for the possibility that Hess, and his Nazi henchmen, slipped unobtrusively into either La Plata or Buenos Aires. The reason for sending him to Argentina was for vetting and interrogation by a committee whose commanding SS general was known to be a fanatic, dyed-in-the-wool, Nazi zealot with strong views about the future of his defeated regime and the treatment of deserters from the 'cause.' It is almost certain that this bigoted Nazi 'commander' would not have believed Hess's arrogant assertions that he was indeed the Deputy Führer and a Colonel General in Henrich Himmler's SS Standarte. The mock 'Tribunal's' conclusion would inevitably be that '*Herr* Ernst Prost' was a spy implanted in their midst by British Intelligence. In their book, this was a treasonable offence, which carried the death penalty. That the man before them could be the real McCoy might have crossed their minds but the 'Commander' would have reminded his committee of Adolf Hitler's edict when Hess defected in 1941 -- "He (Hess) is a traitor to be shot on sight if he returns to the Fatherland." In either event the 'cowboy Tribunal' would have condemned '*Herr* Prost', or more accurately Rudolf Hess, to death. Where the final act could have been perpetrated will always remain one of life's longstanding mysteries. There are a series of deep lakes and reservoirs to the south of Buenos Aires. One of these would have made a likely resting place for Rudolf Hess, the second most important Nazi in Germany's Third Reich in the 1930s.

For months after 'Prost's' disappearance into thin air the British Government kept pressing embassies in Montevideo and Buenos Aires to leave no stone unturned in their investigations into 'Prost's' defection. Prime Minister Attlee was fully aware what might happen at the Nuremberg Trial if, as it seemed certain, Hess's impostor was condemned to death and he would be forced to reveal his true identity. The Government would have to own up to the Maindiff 'switch' and to the extradition of the 'real' Hess to Uruguay. The P.M. could not bear thinking about the outcome if he had to declare to the world that his Government had mislaid a most important Nazi prisoner and that the 'Hess' who stood trial at Nuremberg was, in fact, an impostor.

The International Military Tribunal announced its verdict on the 1st of October 1946. The man in the dock, purporting to be Rudolf Hess, was given a life sentence. Attlee and MI6 fully expected Prost to declare his true identity but, much to their surprise, he declined to do so. He readily accepted a life sentence on behalf of his revered Deputy Führer and continued with the charade until, at 92 years of age, he allegedly terminated his own life at Spandau Prison, Berlin in August 1987.

Successive British governments have been reluctant to reveal the truth about the identity of the prisoner who stood in the dock on behalf of Rudolf Hess. In the first three decades of Prost's incarceration, during the Cold War, the Russians were the chief stumbling block in agreeing to release Prisoner No. 7 in Spandau on compassionate grounds. Their basic reason for conforming to Hess's life sentence was to allow their troops, and secret agents, free access into West Berlin during their dedicated months' guard duty at Spandau Prison, as ordered by the War Crimes Commissionaires at Nuremberg. As Soviet influence in Western Europe declined at the end of the Cold War, so did their attitude towards Hess's release and, from the mid-1970's, the British Government became the main antagonists to his discharge from Spandau Prison. The British reason for their policy towards Prisoner No. 7 almost certainly hinges around the fact that Hess's senior family members and Nazi Party colleagues were either dead or too senile and incapable of positively identifying Rudolf Hess. In all probability it may also account for the Government's disinclination to allow DNA studies on his exhumed remains, which might have established his true identity once and for all. Ernst Prost had continued with the deception for 41 years before his death and Britain saw no reason to reopen the identity controversy. It may be that their objective to this very day is to maintain a status quo and let sleeping dogs lie.

THE INTERNATIONAL MILITARY TRIBUNAL-NUREMBERG

NOVEMBER 1945 – OCTOBER 1946

Prime Minister Winston Churchill, America's President Franklin D. Roosevelt and Russia's Communist dictator, Joseph Stalin, met in conference at Yalta in February 1945 and the fate of Germany's Nazi leaders at the conclusion of World War II was high on the agenda. Italy had already surrendered to the Allies in September 1943 and, a month later, declared war on her one-time Axis partner. Britain and America insisted on a non-negotiable, unconditional surrender from Germany and a trial for war crimes of the most prominent military and political Nazis. Churchill and Roosevelt had great difficulty in convincing 'Uncle Joe' that not all Nazi leaders and SS officers should be executed out of hand and without trial. This was understandable at the time as millions of Stalin's countrymen had been murdered by the ruthless Waffen SS. Agreement was reached between the three world leaders that a catalogue of prominent Nazis was to be compiled for a grand showpiece trial at the end of hostilities. The Palace of Justice in the Bavarian city of Nuremberg was selected for this legal charade and most, if not all, Nazi war criminals scheduled to appear in court were almost certain to hang for their nefarious wartime activities. Nuremberg had close connections with Hitler's National Socialist Party and was a centre for Nazi Party rallies in the 1930s. Four Allied nations, now including France, were to provide teams of legal and medical experts for the prosecution and the arraigned Nazi prisoners were assigned German advocates for their own defence.

At the end of the European conflict Germany was partitioned into Eastern and Western Zones and Nuremberg came under the American theatre of influence. Consequently, duties for administrating the Tribunal and for guarding the prisoners fell to the Americans. Colonel Burton C. Andruss was appointed Prison Commandant and U.S. Military Police, known as 'snowdrops' for their habit of wearing white helmets, belts and gaiters, were entrusted with guarding the prisoners. The Nuremberg trial judges, advocates and court officials convened at the end of October 1945 and the Trial itself started sitting on the 20th of November. The hearing lasted eleven months and their verdict was announced on the 1st of October 1946. The world then learnt the fate of the principal Nazi leaders who perpetrated such heinous acts during their reign in power in the 1930s and during World War II.

A Four-Power War Crimes Commission was set up in February 1945 to identify those Nazis who would be indicted for trial at Nuremberg. The Russians, and to a certain extent the French, wanted to include all senior military figures, the Gestapo and S.S. officers, in a list of over a thousand wartime criminals. This was plainly impracticable and, eventually, two categories of miscreants were identified. In Category I around forty names were agreed should appear at a showpiece trial in Nuremberg. Category II cases, of around 400 in number, were scheduled to be tried in Courts spread throughout Germany. By the time the Nuremberg Tribunal was in session the number of Category I prisoners had been whittled down to 27 and Rudolf Hess was a prominent name on the list of indictees. Adolf Hitler and Joseph Göebbels had committed suicide in the

Führerbunker in Berlin. After his capture by the British in north Germany Heinrich Himmler committed suicide by taking cyanide and Martin Bormann was presumed to be dead by the time the War Crimes Tribunal was in session. These four leading Nazis were tried in absentia and condemned to death. Twenty-three high-ranking Nazis were in prison at the Palace of Justice by the second week of October 1945, a number reduced by one when Robert Ley hung himself in his cell a week after his arrival in Nuremberg.

The main Court Room in the Palace of Justice occupied the centre of the ground floor and the prisoners' separate cells were on the first and second floors of the building. Communication between the prisoners in their cells was strictly forbidden and enforced by the presence of U.S. Military Police 'Snowdrops' outside each cell day and night. Restrictions on the prisoners were rigidly applied at first but, within a couple of weeks, they were granted certain liberties. Reading and writing materials became available and they were allowed free access to their attorneys. At mealtimes a reasonable choice was offered and recognition was paid to their dietary requirements. The Nazi prisoners were treated with due deference by the warders and military staff but they were never referred to by their titles or surnames. Prost was placed in a cell on the first floor and, assigned by his cell number, became Convict 125.

On the day of his admission to the Palace of Justice, Prost was subjected to a thorough medical examination by Captain Ben Horewitz of the U.S. Army Medical Corps. Horewitz reported two recent, one-inch scars on the prisoner's chest wall, the legacy of a surgical procedure carried out on Prost in August 1945 to simulate the self-inflicted stab wounds Rudolf Hess had sustained at Maindiff Court Hospital the previous

February. The medical officer's thorough examination did not reveal any larger scars on the front, or back, of the prisoner's chest to suggest he had sustained a serious gunshot wound in 1917 during World War I. Prost's Luftwaffe uniform was taken away and stored and he was issued with standard prison clothing -- grey slacks, a blue shirt and a plain gabardine jacket. For courtroom appearances prisoners were fitted with dark-blue suits and white shirts. During their first few weeks in Nuremberg they were constantly shepherded by an American prison guard and contact with Nazi colleagues was avoided. Prost spent most of his time in solitary confinement in his cell. The showpiece Trial commenced in earnest on the 20th of November and restrictions were relaxed to a certain extent. The prisoners were now allowed to converse among themselves in the dining hall at mealtimes, at the twice-weekly bathing parade and, to a lesser extent, during their daily exercise sessions. White-helmeted 'Snowdrop' prison guards were present in the background on all these occasions, one guard to one prisoner.

Leaning on his thespian background Ernst Prost took to acting dumb and playing up his amnesia in his chance meetings with his Nazi co-conspirators. On the other hand they reacted indifferently towards him and tended to give him a wide berth at their communal mealtimes and in the exercise yard. A few of Rudolf Hess's former Party colleagues were openly hostile towards Prisoner 125 and regarded him as a deserter, at least, or a traitor, at most, to the Nazi regime. This suited Prost down to the ground and, when anyone deigned to speak to him, his replies were usually monosyllabic. When questioned about shared experiences in Germany before the war Prost fell back on his trusted defence, claiming he could not remember the occasion or the event. One day in the dining hall Hermann

Göering approached Prost about a Berlin reception for Benito Mussolini and Count Ciano at which they had both been present. Prost alleged he had no memory of the event and had never heard of the Italian dictator and his Foreign Minister. In early November the prison authorities brought Professor Karl Haushofer for a meeting with Prisoner 125 in his cell. The professor had been Rudolf Hess's personal tutor and mentor during his student days at Munich University and was involved in planning the Deputy Führer's flight to Britain. When they met in his cell Prost was apologetic and said he was sorry but he could not remember ever meeting Haushofer. It is hard to imagine the ageing professor did not recognise him as an impostor, which speaks volumes for Prost's ability to mimic Rudolf Hess to a tee. In 1945 Professor Haushofer was under protective custody by the U.S. military. Communist secret agents were agitating to secure his transference to a Russian detention centre where his execution as a Nazi agent would be a certainty. The old professor might have realised Prost was an impostor but he declined to reveal his suspicions to the Nuremberg advocates. Four months after his visit to the Palace of Justice Professor Haushofer could no longer bear the brunt of confinement and menacing pressure by Russian secret agents. Then, on March 11th 1946, together with his half-Jewish wife, Martha, he took a lethal dose of poison in the woods near their home. Martha also had the strength to hang herself.

Similarly, Rudolf Hess's long-term female secretaries, Hildegard Fath and Inga Spree were presented to Prisoner No. 125 in November and, much to the chagrin of the ladies, Prost apologised and stated he could not remember working with them. On a few occasions Joachim von Ribbentrop claimed that Prisoner No. 125 was not the Rudolf Hess he had known, and worked with, in Germany in the 1930s. Ribbentrop was in a good position to know the facts about Rudolf Hess as they had a close relationship in Foreign Affairs before the outbreak of World War II. They collaborated in the successful, bloodless Austrian 'anschluss', the freeing of Sudeten Germans in Czechoslovakia in 1938, and organising resistance from German nationals in Danzig before Hitler's invasion of Poland on the 1st September 1939. Taking advantage of his supposed loss of memory Prost played the amnesia game to perfection and blankly denied he had ever met Joachim von Ribbentrop. Herman Göering was aggressive towards Prost in Court and openly queried the identity of the man sitting on his left side in the Dock. The prison authorities inexplicably disregarded Göering's outbursts and did not investigate his allegations

Some of the Nazi convicts in Nuremberg were prepared to extend a hand in friendship towards Prost. Albert Speer, Hitler's closest confidant and co-organiser with Rudolf Hess of the pre-war Nuremberg rallies, became himself a persona non grata among his Nazi colleagues and was a kindred spirit. Acting the part Prost convinced Speer he could not remember their collaboration in planning the rallies and could not even recall working with him. Speer had other pressures on his mind throughout the Trial. He had to plead for mercy from the Tribunal to save his own skin and there was little time to delve into Prisoner No. 125's infuriating memory loss. Walter Funk, the *Reichsminister* for Economics, had collaborated closely with Rudolf Hess in financing Nazi Party projects. Funk was in a permanent quandary, and always ready to discuss with anyone who cared to listen, why he had been indicted in the first place. Funk considered he was innocent on all charges and, like Speer, he was only interested in his own predicament. A leader of the

Hitler Youth movement in the 1930s, Baldur von Schirach shared his headquarters with Hess in the Braunhaus in Munich. During the war, the Führer made him Gauleiter of Vienna. He was a staunch Nazi and conducted himself correctly towards his colleagues at the Palace of Justice. Von Schirach would have known Hess in Munich in the 1930s but, by the end of the war, his eyesight was failing and he had no reason to disbelieve Convict No.125 was not Rudolf Hess in person.

Every one of the twenty-two accused Nazis on trial in November 1945 was allocated a defence lawyer and a well-established attorney, Dr Seidl, was appointed to represent Prost. Dr Seidl rapidly became disillusioned by his plaintiff's loss of memory and he was hampered in preparing a solid brief for Prisoner 125's defence. He saw a legal loophole and requested psychiatric opinions about his client's mental fitness to testify before the Tribunal. Two eminent American psychiatrists examined Prost a week before the trial commenced. Major Douglas M Keilly and Dr Donald Euan Cameron, an expert on the treatment of amnesia, formed an opinion that Prost was suffering from 'prison psychosis,' hysteria and paranoia but judged he was fit to testify before the War Crimes Tribunal. Strangely, the opinions of the British psychiatrists, Majors Dicks and Ellis Jones, were not sought in this matter, despite the fact the latter specialist had been Rudolf Hess's personal mental health carer at Maindiff Court Hospital for over three years.

The War Crimes Tribunal sat for the first time on the 20th of November 1945. Dressed in dark suits and white shirts the defendants were seated in two tiers in the dock. Prost sat in the front row with Hermann Göering, wearing dark glasses, in pole position on his right and Joachim von Ribbentrop on his left side. Prost's seating position in Court was an indication that he was still regarded as the second most important Nazi on trial. The entire Court and defendants were supplied with headphones and immediate translation into German, English, French and Russian was available. Prost sat staring vacantly into space and when asked to plead he remained silent. Dr Seidl was forced to answer a plea of 'not guilty' on his behalf. Dr Seidl then made out a case that Prisoner 125 was guilty of signing decrees on behalf of the Nazi Party but, more often than not, he had no formal input into establishing the laws. Seidl played down his client's influence in Foreign Affairs and in recruiting German nationals to act for the Party. Rudolf Hess's high rank in the SS was cited as merely a token appointment and he definitely had no dealings with the Gestapo. Prost play-acted in dock to the limits of his capability. When asked a direct question he would either remain silent, or plead a lack of memory. Sometimes he embarked on an irrelevant tirade which had little bearing on the cross-questioning under consideration. This attitude plainly infuriated his co-defendants and led to pointed remarks from his colleagues. They felt that Hess was making a mockery of a Trial which, for the majority, meant life or death.

By February 1946 Prost had dismissed his personal attorney and announced he was undertaking his own defence. Dr Seidl was probing too deeply into Rudolf Hess's past actions about which Prost had only scanty knowledge. Ready answers were not forthcoming from Prisoner No. 125 and pleading amnesia was wearing a bit thin. He now had carte blanche to answer the prosecuting attorneys as he thought fit and loss of memory got him out of replying to many tricky situations. When a film of the horrors of the holocaust was shown in Court in November Prost sat through the ordeal blank-faced, afterwards denying any knowledge about, or involvement in, anti-Semitic activities. He then withdrew into his shell and was sometimes excused attendance at Court hearings. It is highly probable that Ernst Prost, and possibly Rudolf Hess, would have been emotionally upset by the horrendous images of human suffering witnessed in the holocaust film. By now Hermann Göering was criticising Prisoner No. 125 and voiced his objections in Court and, more volubly, in the dining hall. As a result Göering was made to partake of his meals in the privacy of his own cell. Prost derived pleasure in goading Göering and von Ribbentrop, his two main behavioural critics. It satisfied him to think he was repaying his mentor, Rudolf Hess, for the anguish the two had caused his master when the Nazis were in power in Germany in the 1930s.

In August 1946 the Tribunal was reaching its decision. Ernst Prost was certain he faced a death sentence and, in that case, he would be forced to declare his identity to get off the hook. He was determined to go out with a bang and, with all flags flying, to create a lasting impression on the Tribunal and the World Press. Prost prepared a long and rambling address which, much to the Tribunal's and his co-defendants' surprise, he delivered at a summing-up session at the Palace of Justice on the 31st of August 1946. Prost's closing statement lasted 40 minutes and the gist of his speech dealt with the unfairness of the Treaty of Versailles, the need for lebensraum for the German people, the dangers of Bolshevism in Europe and Jewish infiltration into major industries and banking institutions. He again denied any knowledge of Concentration Camps in Germany and the holocaust. He then declared his enduring loyalty to Adolf Hitler, the greatest man Germany, and the World, had ever known. Expecting a death sentence, and with tongue in cheek, Ernst Prost ended his statement dramatically:

"I shall appear before the Tribunal of the Almighty. I shall answer to Him, and Him alone, and I know He will absolve me."

Russia's senior Tribunal member, General Rodenko, immediately asked for a death sentence. The other three Allied Powers opted for life imprisonment and, in Convict 125's case, it literally meant "life."

The seven Nazis who received custodial sentences were - Ernst Prost, alias Rudolf Hess, Walter Funk and Grand Admiral Erich Raeder – life; Albert Speer and Baldur von Schirach – 20 years; Baron Constantin von Neurath – 15 years and Kreigsmarine Admiral Karl Doenitz – 10 years.

Ivone Kirkpatrick of MI6 and Prime Minister Attlee's Private Secretary were at the Palace of Justice to witness the Tribunal's judgment on the 1st of October. Seated in a public gallery at the back of the courtroom they observed the proceedings with fascination. When it came to Prost's turn to stand in the dock for sentencing they were amazed he avoided the death penalty. No one was more surprised than Prost himself on hearing his fate. He had been convinced beforehand he would be for hanging and now he had to rethink his position. Prost had enjoyed the drama and limelight of acting in court and he had made a meal of impersonating Rudolf Hess. The satisfaction he had derived from the exercise in deception helped him to make up his mind about his future. Continuing with his imprisonment would at least, allow him to rub shoulders with six notorious, convicted Nazi war criminals who once graced the corridors of power in Adolf Hitler's Third Reich. It was a chance in a lifetime for a down-and-out actor who had no other prospects in a destitute post-war Germany. Ernst had succeeded in getting away with fooling the War Crimes Tribunal and his Nazi brethren. His prospects outside the prison walls had little to offer and his likeness to Rudolf Hess would make him a marked man in society. He reasoned the safest place for the time being was in prison where he could continue play-acting the part of Rudolf Hess, free of interference from the outside world. The British authorities fully expected Prost to reveal his true identity after sentencing. If Prost had done so the convoluted plans to explain the disappearance of the 'true' Rudolf Hess would have to come into effect. Prime Minister Atlee decided to wait and see how far down the road Prost would continue with the deception. At that moment Attlee's government had the luxury of not getting egg on their faces by having to disclose to the world that the "Hess," who stood in the witness box at Nuremberg and was awarded a life sentence, was not Rudolf Hess but Ernst Prost, a vaudeville actor and a butcher's adopted son from Munich.

The seven Nazi war criminals were kept in separate cells at the Palace of Justice in Nuremberg until the 18th of August 1947. Ernst Prost revelled in maintaining his deception. He continued to complain of psychosomatic symptoms and his paranoia and amnesia had re-established themselves full-time. He refused to meet Rudolf Hess's family; he even refused to have blood taken for grouping; he refused to give a specimen signature and he refused to sign a dollar bill for one of the guards. His fellow inmates, by and large, remained aloof and still regarded him as a deserter from the Nazi cause. Albert Speer was also sidelined by his colleagues. They regarded Speer as a turncoat who let the side down by admitting to the Court the existence of Concentration Camps and the ethnic cleansing programme. He had proclaimed at the Tribunal that it was common knowledge in Germany in 1943. Relieved by escaping the gallows Speer and Walter Funk became friendlier with Prost though Funk spent most of his time complaining about the severity of his life sentence.

Russian pressure at Four Power meetings insisted the Nazi convicts' permanent prison had to be sited in Berlin. Reluctantly the three remaining Western Powers agreed. The eastern half of the city was under Communist control of the East German Government. Spandau Prison, in the British Charlottenberg district of West Berlin, was selected and, by August 1947, was ready to receive Ernst Prost and his six Nazi compatriots. Cell No. 7 at Spandau gaol now became Prost's 'home' for the ensuing 41 years and, for the last 21 years of his life, he was the sole occupant of Spandau prison which, in its heyday, could accommodate up to 600 convicted criminals.

PRISONER NO. 7'S TWILIGHT YEARS AT SPANDAU

NOVEMBER 1969 - AUGUST 1987

Following the Nuremberg Tribunal, arrangements for the seven Nazi prisoners at Spandau met with Russian and East German approval, allowing free access to their troops and secret agents into West Berlin. Armed Russians provided monthly guards once a quarter at Spandau gaol and they also stood on 24-hour guard duty at the Monument to Fallen Heroes erected in the British Sector in the Tiergarten, a quarter of a mile away from the Brandenburg Gate.

By the summer of 1957 four of Spandau's seven prisoners had been released. Walter Funk, in 1957, and Grand Admiral Raeder, in 1955, had had their life sentences annulled; Baron von Neurath was released on compassionate grounds also in 1955 with 5 years of his sentence to run, and Karl Doenitz had served his 10 years in jail in full. In consequence, there was a hue and cry for "Hess's" release under the same umbrella. As might be expected the Russians vehemently refused permission and the British response in favour was surprisingly lukewarm. Between May 1957 and December 1966 only three prisoners remained in captivity in Spandau and repeated appeals for clemency for Prisoner No. 7 fell on deaf ears. In December 1966 Baldur von Schirach and Albert Speer were set free having completed their twenty-year sentences and this consigned Prisoner No. 7 to sole occupancy of the prison for the rest of his life. At that time a concerted effort was again made to secure

"Hess's" release, with the United States and France strongly in favour. The U.S.S.R. was dead against such a move and, curiously enough, Britain acted as an honest broker between the two factions, paying lip service to No. 7's release and secretly lending support to the Russian veto. U.S.S.R. politicians held strong convictions that Rudolf Hess had been a prime orchestrator of Operation Barbarossa, the German attack on Russia in June 1941, a claim that was entirely untrue. They also harboured thoughts that Hess had flown to Britain by invitation of the British Secret Service. It might be speculative to assume that, for their own good reasons, the British Government did not wish to condone "Hess's" passage to freedom -- and to reveal his true identity.

A major crisis happened in November 1969 when Prisoner No. 7 was admitted to the British Military Hospital with a suspected perforated peptic ulcer. The symptoms started on the 19th of November during the Russian duty month. A week's delay ensued before the Russians agreed to transfer No. 7 to the B.M.H. A barium meal X-Ray examination was not successful but it did demonstrate an intact stomach. A subsequent chest X-Ray showed air under the diaphragm, proving the stomach had leaked at some stage but the perforation had sealed itself without surgical intervention and Prost was treated medically along conservative lines.

On admission to the B.M.H. Prisoner No. 7 was near death's door and was persuaded to see "Hess's" family for the first time in 28 years. Hess's wife, Ilse, and his only son, Wolf Rüdiger, visited him recovering at the B.M.H. on Christmas Eve 1969. They saw a frail, white-faced, cadaveric man with sunken cheeks and glazed eyes lying on a bed and receiving a blood transfusion. Wolf Rüdiger was barely four when his father flew to Britain and only had vague memories of his parent. Now, nearly seventy years of age, Ilse Hess was dubious but convinced herself the scarecrow of a man in the hospital bed was her husband. She persuaded Wolf Rüdiger in the same belief. Defying all odds Prost made a complete recovery, and after six weeks in hospital, he was returned to his lonely cell in Spandau. It is of interest to note that when Prisoner No. 7 was in the hospital for six weeks Russian guards insisted on keeping watch on the unoccupied gaol, a sure indication of their determination to maintain their legal entry channels into West Berlin open at all costs.

After the 1969 crisis Prisoner No. 7 sank into semi-obscurity and was consigned to the backwater. Thirty-two year old Wolf Rüdiger Hess and Dr Seidl, his personal advocate at Nuremberg, made strenuous efforts to secure his release and approached the Allied Governments and the European Commission for Human Rights. They wrote letters to the Press from time to time but all their efforts came up against a blank wall, mainly due to the intransigency of the Russian Government. Family visits to Spandau Prison were now allowed once a month. Frau Ilse Hess only paid a visit on rare occasions between 1970 and 1987. She complained the visits were too stressful and she could not face meeting with her 'husband' in the forbidding prison environment. It is equally probable she found communication with Prisoner No. 7 difficult and he did not respond to her in the warm manner she had known 28 years previously, before Hess's flight to Britain in May 1941. Frau Isle Hess survived to the ripe old age of 95 and, until her death on 7th September 1995, she was convinced that Prisoner No.7 in Spandau was her husband. An American officer, Colonel Eugene Bird, had been appointed Prison

Director in 1968. His main ambition in life was to write a book about Germany's National Socialist Party and, for this purpose, he solicited cooperation from Prisoner No. 7. Prost called on all his acting ability to string Colonel Bird along for months on end. As an example, many hours were spent on No. 7's knowledge about Operation Barbarossa. The Colonel was aware that Rudolf Hess had been a member of Hitler's Secret War Cabinet but Prost insisted he rarely attended meetings and definitely did not know Barbarossa's commencement date. And for this seemingly gratuitous information Colonel Bird made arrangements for No. 7 to have a more comfortable lifestyle in prison. He was moved from Cell No. 7 into larger accommodation in the former prison chapel on the ground floor at Spandau. The prison staff became more sympathetic to his needs and allowed him extra time in bed in the mornings. On their quarterly duty months even the Russian orderlies and warders bent the Nuremberg Commissioners' rules and helped to make No. 7's daily prison routine less stressful. A permanent guard was stationed in the corridor outside his "new" cell and his door was left unlocked throughout the day allowing Prost free access down the corridor to a private toilet and bathroom. If he so desired he was at liberty to have daily showers. These relaxations in prison routine only applied to the immediate surroundings of his cell. It was a strict prison rule that he was never permitted to go unaccompanied either to the exercise yard or anywhere else inside the prison precincts.

By now Prost was receiving regular monthly visits from Rudolf Hess's family. These visits were strictly controlled and overseen by two or three prison officials. They saw to it that human contact did not occur at any time and references to the Nazi regime and the Third Reich were banned. Prost had permission to write a heavily censored letter to Hess's family and friends once a month, to keep up-to-date with newssheets, to listen to radio broadcasts and music, and he had free access to a well-stocked prison library. He was encouraged to exercise two or three times a day, always with a prison warder in close attendance. As the years slipped by his wearisome daily routine never varied and his days were mainly spent reading in the library, and in his cell, and exercising in the outdoor compound. As a legacy of the Cold War, prison restrictions were only marginally relaxed during the Russian duty month and Prost came to welcome supervision by the other three Allied Powers. It is of significance to note that Prisoner No. 7 attempted to commit suicide by cutting his wrists with a table knife during a harsh Russian duty month in February 1977. His failed attempt led to a return to 24-hour vigilance by the guards and warders. Restrictions only lasted for two months and were given up in favour of the previous relaxed regime practised by the British, French and American guardians.

In his early days at Spandau Hess's impostor had been fit and agile and perfectly capable of joining his Nazi colleagues in the exercise compound and garden. He only did so rarely and he was usually accompanied Albert Speer on his ritual exercise hikes. Prost became the sole prisoner in Spandau in December 1966 and his attitude changed completely. He looked forward to his daily exercise periods. Disaster struck in November 1969 when his stomach ulcer perforated. He came out of the B.M.H a wizened, debilitated 75-year-old man and, though he was to live for another 18 years, his physical condition went gradually downhill from that time onwards. A common complication of the ageing process is the development of atherosclerosis, a hardening of the arteries, leading to a high blood pressure and vascular complications. In the early 70s Prisoner No. 7 had suffered from a slight stroke, which left him with a weakness of his left arm and impaired grip in his left hand. Like Hess, Prost was left-handed and this disability caused difficulty in writing and gripping objects. As the years progressed his eyesight deteriorated and, due to his hypertension, he began losing his sense of balance. So much so he was unable to negotiate stairs unaided. Another medical condition allied to senility is osteoporosis and Prisoner No. 7 had a fixed forward stoop and limited restriction of his head movements. By the time 92-year-old No. 7 came to his ultimate end he showed the common, and regrettably inevitable, result of the ageing process -- he was a bent, staggering and stooping figure with limited vision and he walked with a shuffling, unsteady gait. Aided by a walking stick, and supported by a warder, he was still able to negotiate his way around the exercise compound and, weather permitting, he enjoyed the virtues of walking in the open air.

Prisoner No. 7's definitive, and successful, suicide occurred at around 3.30pm on the 17th August 1987, and details of the tragic event are well documented. That he intended taking his own life on that day in question is not in dispute. A suicide note was found in his jacket pocket at the post mortem examination two days after the event and his writing was confirmed to be authentic by a handwriting expert. The official version concerning the reason for No. 7's suicide was the appointment of a black warder, one Anthony Jordan, to look after his needs. It does not hold water. An impostor would not necessarily have the same extreme racial prejudices as the real Rudolf Hess. Prisoner No. 7 did not show any antagonism towards his black helper and they were on friendly terms. To continue with the deception to the very end the suicide note discovered at autopsy requested the prison governor to forward Prost's letter to Hess's wife, Ilse, thanking her for all she had done and tried to do for him during his extensive years in captivity. It was hardly the death wish of a devoted husband.

The seventeenth of August 1987 started normally for Prisoner No. 7 with a morning walk after breakfast and a two-hour siesta after a light lunch. Clothed in a white shirt, grey flannels with red braces and a light-blue jacket, Prost was escorted into the exercise yard by Anthony Jordan at 2.30pm.They were seen by a G.I. prison guard, sitting on a garden seat in earnest conversation at around three o'clock. Shortly afterwards Jordan led No. 7 into the garden shed, hidden by tall trees from the guards' watchtower sentry post. The garden hut was a rectangular wooden structure used as a depository by the prison staff and cluttered with tools and gardening implements. The floor was covered by a layer of dust, wood-shavings and metal filings. Electricians had left coils of yellow electric flex near the doorway. A solid workbench was positioned along one wall and half a dozen folding, wooden chairs were stacked against the opposite sidewall. By a special concession No. 7 was allowed to sit on one of the chairs to rest his weary limbs or to shelter from a rain shower.

Official accounts of Prisoner No. 7's suicide, and the subsequent Special Branch investigation and autopsy by a British pathologist, have been widely published and recorded for posterity. At around 3.15pm on the 17th of August No. 7 was seated in his usual position in the shed when Jordan was called away to answer a mystery telephone call in the central office block. He left Prost to sit alone in the garden hut depository. To leave a prisoner to his own devices was strictly against prison regulations and Jordan was never asked to explain why he did so and what was the content of the mysterious phone call. On returning 15 minutes later the black warder found No. 7 half-laying on the floor, propped against the work bench with his knees drawn up to his chest and his trousers covered with dust, wood chippings and metal filings. Prost's face was blue and a length of yellow electric flex was hanging from a window fitting and tied tightly around his neck. Jordan raised the alarm and help appeared quickly from all directions. Someone cut the flex to release No. 7 from the noose around his neck. He was then dragged outside onto a grass verge and attempts were made to revive him by mouth-to-mouth resuscitation and external cardiac massage. The latter procedure was undertaken by untrained persons and resulted in fractures to six osteoporotic ribs on the left side of No. 7's chest and three ribs on the right. In the middle of the frantic activity at the grass verge outside the hut a stretcher appeared out of nowhere and Prost was bundled on to it. He was then manhandled through the central cellblock and across the drawbridge to the main prison entrance where a military ambulance was waiting for the stretcher party. Attempts were made on the ambulance to administer oxygen to the patient but the endotracheal tube was misplaced into Prost's gullet and only resulted in inflating his stomach. The ambulance covered the two-mile dash down *Herrstrasse* in nine minutes and, despite further attempts at resuscitation at the B.M.H, the hospital staff declared Prisoner No. 7 dead at 4.35pm. Prost's body was taken to the mortuary. He was fully clothed and the endotracheal tube was still in position. Allegedly no photographs were taken of the corpse at any time after his admission to the B.M.H.

A hasty Four-Power emergency meeting was convened on the evening of No. 7's admission to hospital. The conference ended in confusion with the Russian delegates blaming the American prison staff for lack of proper supervision of Spandau's important prisoner.

By 1987 Russia's attitude towards No. 7's release was changing and, in September 1986, Mikael Gorbachev, then General Secretary of the Soviet Communist Party, had publicly announced a proposed amnesty for "Hess." The British Government were slow in responding to the olive branch extended by the U.S.S.R. The reason for Britain's tardiness at this stage remains a mystery. One likely suggestion is that, having shielded Prost's true identity for 42 years, they feared he might come clean and stir up a hornet's nest at a time when relationships between Britain and the U.S.S.R. were improving.

The British delegates now took over complete control of the Four-Power meeting and the Russian officers left in a huff. A British pathologist was elected to carry out an autopsy and investigation into No. 7's suspected suicide was delegated to the Special Investigation Branch, the S.I.B, of the Royal Military Police. S.I.B's task was severely hampered from the start by the chaotic conditions inside the garden hut, a result of the frantic attempts by the prison staff to resuscitate "Hess." A tell-tale strand of electric flex was found in a tangled heap on the floor, trodden-on and covered by dust and wood chippings. For a reason best known to themselves S.I.B. failed to interview the black warder in attendance on Prisoner No. 7 at the time of the incident and neglected to ascertain why Anthony Jordan left his post in the garden shed unattended. On inspection of the body the S.I.B. agents were denied permission to undress the corpse and either to take photographs or, more pertinently, to fingerprint the cadaver. By the next day the Special Branch team had arrived at a conclusion that Prisoner No. 7 had taken his own life and committed suicide by hanging.

A London University professor, and senior Army Pathologist, had been instructed years previously that, one day, he might be called upon to perform an autopsy on the remaining Nazi in Spandau. Professor J.M. Cameron flew into Berlin on the evening of the 18th of August and conducted his autopsy in the presence of a hoard of Four-Power observers on the following day. Available for his inspection were X-Ray plates of the entire body and S.I.B.'s report into their investigations and conclusions as to the cause of death. Prisoner No. 7 still wore the clothes he had worn in the garden hut and, during undressing, a suicide note was unexpectedly found in the right-hand pocket of his blue-grey jacket. This startling finding might have prejudiced the eventual autopsy outcome. On the left side of the corpse's neck there was bruising and a three-inch 'fine linear scar,' evidence of the pressure exerted by the electric flex. On the front of his left chest two superficial one-inch scars were recorded – evidence of the self-inflicted stab wounds made by Rudolf Hess in Maindiff Court in February 1945 and replicated on his impostor in August the same year. No other scars were recorded on the dead man's torso. The autopsy did not reveal evidence the corpse had suffered a through-and-through bullet wound to his left chest in World War I. This negative report adds valuable supportive testimony that Prisoner No. 7 in Spandau was not Rudolf Hess but an impostor.

At the autopsy numerous bruises around the cadaver's rib cage were attributed to the heavy pummelling No. 7 received during resuscitation at Spandau and at the B.M.H. One larger bruise under the scalp was attributed to No. 7 striking the back of his head on the workbench as he slid to the ground. Professor

Cameron entered the cause of death as "Asphyxia; Compression of neck; Suspension." Relying on the note found on the corpse's clothing the British Press had no hesitation in reporting Prisoner No. 7 had committed suicide by hanging. What the Press did not realise, and certain members of the British Government and MI6 might have known for a fact, the victim of the suicide they were reporting was to an impostor and not to the "real" Rudolf Hess.

The British Government had made pre-mortem plans for No. 7's burial many years before his eventual death on the 17th of August. To avoid his grave becoming a shrine for would-be Nazi worshippers in future years they made arrangements for cremating "Hess" immediately after his death. International pressure forced the Government to hand over No.7's body to the Hess Family for burial. The family opted for interment at a secret plot in the Fitchel Mountains in Franconia. Prost's body was taken from Berlin by air to its destination on the 20th of August and received by Wolf Rüdiger and Dr. Seidl, Hess's long-term legal adviser since the Nuremberg Tribunal. Not satisfied with the Berlin verdict they ordered a second private autopsy, which was carried out on the 21st of August by a Professor W. Spann from Munich University. An eminent pathologist, Spann's findings did not vary to any significant degree from Professor Cameron's conclusions. It is noteworthy that the German professor also did not record scars or any evidence the body he was dissecting had been shot through the left chest in World War I. Professor Spann concluded No. 7's death had not been natural and had been caused by "a strangling instrument around the throat". The strangling instrument in this case was the yellow, electric flex and the victim's ensuing death was almost certainly attributable to self-inflicted suicide by hanging.

That Prisoner No. 7's death might be reclassified in future as euthanasia is open to controversy and doubt, and speculation on the matter continues to emerge. Abdallah Melaouhi was the prison's resident male nurse and he had tended to Prisoner No 7 for over five years. He knew No 7's physical capabilities and, a few weeks after "Hess's" tragic death, he testified that his patient at Spandau did not have the strength, or mobility, to commit suicide. Melaouhi did not consider No. 7 capable of climbing on to a wooden chair unaided and he definitely did not possess the manual dexterity to manipulate the yellow flex into a noose and tether it to a window fixture above his head. The implication of Melaouhi's sworn evidence is that Prisoner No. 7 was either assisted to hang himself or an outside agency might have performed the ritual hanging. American GI guards were seen crossing the exercise compound to their sentry posts at around three o'clock but the most likely explanation is that No. 7 met his end by assisted euthanasia. The part played by Anthony Jordan, No. 7's black warder at the time of his suicide, has not yet been disclosed by the British authorities. Until that day comes we shall not be in possession of the full facts about his final hour at Spandau Prison, be he Rudolf Hess or an impostor.

By the age of 92 Prisoner No.7 had come to the end of his tether and had lost his will to carry on living. Almost totally blind, and riddled with debilitating arthritis, he wanted to end it all but lacked the physical capability to carry out the final act. The author's speculative account of the conspiracy surrounding Prisoner No. 7's 'suicide ' may prove to be not far removed from the truth when MI6's secret details are revealed at a future date. His input into the controversy suggests that, during the

American duty month in April 1987, No. 7 solicited help from Anthony Jordan in arranging his suicide. The black warder dutifully reported the prisoner's request to the American Prison Commandant and was ordered not to speak to anyone about the strange request. The author contends that the American and British Secret Services made a joint decision in April to allow Jordan to go ahead and collaborate with Prisoner No 7's intended course of action. MI6 might have played a major role in covering up No 7's euthanasia as evidenced by the rapid deployment of the Military Police Special Investigation Branch to investigate the suicide and a British Army Pathologist to carry out the autopsy. Plans were also made for No 7's body to be cremated immediately after the autopsy. Jordan was probably assured he would not be subject to investigation if he participated in assisting in Prisoner No 7's euthanasia. No one at any time apparently interviewed Anthony Jordan after No. 7's death.

Prisoner No 7 had written the suicide note to the Hess family a fortnight before the final solution occurred. He thanked Hess's wife, Ilse, for her hard work in attempting to secure his early release from Spandau Prison and the note did not contain any intimate details of their family life together. On the vital day in question Jordan tied one end of the flex to a window fitting. He then physically lifted the frail old man to stand on a garden chair. The other end of the flex was fashioned into a sliding noose and gently tightened around No 7's neck. Jordan held No 7's hand for a few seconds, raised his own hand in salute, turned on his heels and walked out of the hut, ostensibly to receive a mysterious telephone call in the main office block. The black warder returned to the garden hut 15 minutes later to find Prisoner No 7 half-lying, half-sitting on the floor and hanging from the window frame by the strangling electric flex around his neck. He was blue in the face and very probably his life was extinct by the time Jordan returned to the garden hut.

Subsequent happenings lead one to three conclusions and this speculative scenario may represent the sequence of events that occurred in the garden hut at Spandau Prison at around 3:30 pm on the 17th of August. Firstly – the nature and content of the 'urgent' telephone call has never been explained. The most likely answer is that the call was pre-arranged if, in fact, a telephone message was expected at all. The latter explanation fits the bill more accurately and suggests Jordan gave No 7 a time limit to carry out his suicide act and, if he had not done so when the black warder returned to the garden hut, the planned euthanasia would be aborted. As it transpired Rudolf Hess's impostor stepped off the garden chair of his own free will and Warder Jordan had not actively participated in the final, and terminal, act. Secondly, the best person to explain these unanswered discrepancies would be the warder himself but Anthony Jordan was apparently never interviewed by either the Special Branch Investigation team or, subsequently, by the Prison Authorities. A year later Jordan retired from the American Army Prison Service and settled down to live in Berlin. Strangely he did not return to America where he might have been subjected to questioning about the "Hess affair". Rudolf Hess's family firmly believed he had been murdered and the black warder was a key witness in the suicide investigations. Wolf Rüdiger and Dr Seidl, "Hess's" attorney at Nuremberg, made repeated attempts to interview Jordan and the most obstructive authorities to the family's requests were the Foreign Office in London. Thirdly, Prisoner No 7's remains were exhumed twice, once on the 17th March 1988 to remove the cadaver from its secret resting place to a family grave at Wunsiedel, and the second time in August 2011 as a prelude to its cremation. In the family plot at Wunsiedel Prisoner No. 7's headstone was inscribed with the heading *'Ich hab's gewagt'*, translated into English, 'I dared'. The remains' new resting place very soon became an annual rallying point for Nazi worshippers and their unwelcome riotous behaviour became a civil rights issue. Wunsiedel's authorities obtained permission to re-exhume the remains on 20th August 2011 and No. 7's ashes were scattered over the North Sea.

DNA typing came into regular forensic use in the early 1990's and the identity of the corpse might have been established on these two occasions. Rudolf Hess's family twice refused DNA typing of the exhumed remains, a decision apparently supported by the British Foreign Office and covertly backed by MI6 and the American Secret Service.

RUDOLF HESS'S ENIGMAS

R udolf Hess's upbringing was overshadowed by love and adoration from a doting mother, and strict repression by a domineering, Teutonic father whom he venerated from afar. He grew up to be an introspective 'loner' of average intelligence and, all his life, he craved for a father figure to follow and hero-worship. Hess had a distinguished military record in World War 1 and rose to the rank of Lieutenant in the German infantry. Badly wounded in action on 8th August 1917 he made a slow recovery from a gunshot wound to his upper left chest and, in March 1918, he was seconded to the German Imperial Army Air Corps. Trained to fly fighter aircraft and saw four weeks' frontline action before the war ended on 11 November 1918. In January 1920, Hess enrolled at Munich University to study Geopolitics and came under the influence of General Professor Karl Haushofer who immediately became his father figure and remained his mentor throughout his political career in the Third Reich.

Haushofer took Rudolf to a Munich beer hall in 1920 to hear Hitler speak in public and he became transfixed by the messages conveyed by the unkempt music-hall caricature in a shabby, grey mackintosh. Compulsively drawn to Adolf Hitler, he became a lifelong devotee. Hitler's ideals for a German Third Reich became Hess's aim in life and his devotion to his Leader was legendary. Strengthened by the fact he had no personal ambition to displace the Führer, Hess was content to remain Adolf Hitler's lapdog and, when his master became

Chancellor and Dictator of Germany in 1934, Rudolf Hess was appointed Deputy Führer responsible for formulating State legislation and reflecting the wishes and commands of his demonic Leader.

As an administrator Rudolf Hess was indecisive and content to allow others to 'run the show' on his behalf. His main function was to sign Party edicts and to appear at public gatherings, standing beside his Lord and master. He knew that, by lurking in Hitler's shadow, his position within the Party was safe and their close relationship continued until 1937 when he was deposed by the power-hungry *Reichsairmarschal* Hermann Göering. The Führer's determination to take Germany to war to obtain *'lebensraum,'* and at the same time rid the world of Bolshevism, contributed to Hess's demotion. Whereas Hess could deal with internal Party affairs he could not stand mixing with plutocratic Prussian generals who strove to impose their will on his beloved Leader. On the other hand, Hermann Göering stood his ground against the entrenched willpower of the Wehrmacht officers. The Führer's acknowledged expertise in conducting a campaign leading to the fall of France in June 1940 strengthened Göering's position and relegated Hess to the sidelines. Hermann Göering's Luftwaffe failed in their attempt to subjugate the Royal Air Force in the summer of 1940 and Hitler abandoned his plans to invade Britain for the time being. He now turned his eyes eastwards towards Russia. The Wehrmacht generals had fallen into line after the French campaign but a few voices, including Hess's, pointed to the fallacy of conducting a war on two fronts. The Führer agreed that offers for a peace settlement with Britain should be made before his plans for an invasion of the U.S.S.R came to maturity in the summer of 1941.

Adolf Hitler's government was actively seeking a peaceful armistice with Britain immediately after the fall of France in June 1940. Through clandestine channels in Switzerland, Sweden, Spain, and Portugal, British government officials, and MI6 agents, were bombarded with requests from the Nazis for a meeting to discuss peace terms. Britain's wartime Prime Minister, Winston Churchill, steadfastly refused to consider any form of capitulation but paid lip-service to MI6 agents keeping lines open with Germany on the slim chance of discovering Hitler's plans for future conduct of the war and his attitude towards an invasion of Britain.

In July 1940, Adolf Hitler hoped to obtain Britain's surrender and possible cooperation in attacking Soviet Russia. Rudolf Hess offered to fly to England with surrender terms but was denied permission and grounded by the Führer. Negotiations faced a blank wall and Hitler decided to invade Britain. In August 1940 Göering's Luftwaffe were released in a misguided attempt to bring Britain to its knees and as a prelude to an actual invasion by German land and airborne forces. Far from crushing British will power to resist, and aided and abetted by Churchill's rabble-rousing speeches, German bombing raids only served to unite the nation as one and even the sceptics, and those persons who advocated a peace settlement with the Nazis, rallied around the Prime Minister.

By the end of October 1940 Hitler realized Göering's Luftwaffe had fallen far short of its objective and he put the invasion of Britain on hold. He turned his attention to the U.S.S.R. The Führer still harboured hopes Britain would surrender and possibly join him in his planned attack on Russia but the chances of this happening at the height of the London Blitz were virtually nil. By January 1941, Hitler was in tacit agreement that a Nazi bigwig should attempt a meeting with British diplomats on neutral ground. MI6 had been alerted that a high-ranking Nazi official might cross the Channel to the British mainland on the night of 10th May 1941. The War Cabinet was advised about the possible flight and Winston Churchill commented, "Let us await events and see what 'Corporal Schickelgrubber' sends across to see us. Very likely it's another Nazi damp squib." By April 1941, Rudolf Hess was acutely aware of the urgency of an armistice with Britain and for the first time in his life, and without the Führer's consent, he flew across to Scotland on 10th May, ten days before the proposed start date for Operation Barbarossa – the German assault on Soviet Russia. As it transpired Hitler postponed the assault date from May until 22 June 1941 by which time Hess had been a prisoner in England for six weeks.

On 10th May 1941 the plane bearing Rudolf Hess arrived in Scotland and the next day the pilot's identity was confirmed. Churchill was amazed and reacted in typical fashion. He refused to see Hess personally and demanded to be informed of Hitler's peace proposals. More importantly, he ordered the prisoner to be treated as a spy and transferred to the Tower of London with the inevitable implication he would be hung for spying if he did not cooperate with his interrogators. Clement Attlee and his Labour colleagues in the War Cabinet objected to Churchill's impetuous behaviour and forced the Prime Minister to reclassify Hess as an officer prisoner-of-war. He was relocated to a detention centre at Mytchett Place, near Aldershot, where intensive interrogation continued for over a year without any tangible, or worthwhile, results. After Hess's suicide attempt at Mytchett's Camp Z in July 1941 it became evident the Deputy Führer's mental state precluded any valuable information to be forthcoming and Rudolf Hess became a liability and a bone of contention between the Prime Minister and Attlee's Labour faction at the Coalition War Cabinet in Whitehall.

The enigmas surrounding Rudolf Hess revolve, to a large extent, around his mental condition. As a young man he was introspective and moody; in power in the 1930s he was unapproachable and haughty though outwardly polite and correct to his staff and visiting dignitaries; as a prisoner-of-war in Britain between 1941 and 1945 he exhibited paranoia, amnesia and depression with strong suicidal tendencies. All his life Hess had been health conscious and this crystalized into hypochondria in the early 1930s. Disaffected with traditional medicines and qualified doctors Hess began placing his faith in holistic practitioners, herbal cures and astronomy predictions. Most of his symptoms were imagined and, overlying all his complaints, his susceptibility to depressive episodes were often triggered by minor irritations. His demotion in 1938 to No.3 in the Nazi hierarchy hurt Hess more than was evident and his desire to do something to please Adolf Hitler became the overriding factor in his secret decision to fly to Britain in May, 1941. When Hess took off from Augsburg at 5.45pm he was like a dog with two tails on an important mission on behalf of his beloved Fatherland and determined to please his Master and re-establish himself into the Führer's favour. When he parachuted to earth just south of Glasgow at 11.10pm Double British Summer Time he was still in an ebullient mood fortified by his success in navigating his plane a third of the way across hostile territory and landing on British soil in one piece. His Boy Scout elation was soon defused by the British authorities and the darker side of Hess's psyche rapidly became apparent.

After fourteen months at Mytchett Place Hess was transferred to Maindiff Court Hospital in Monmouthshire for the remaining three-and-a-half years of his spell in captivity in Britain. Here he sank into relative obscurity and restrictions on the Nazi prisoner-of-war were considerably relaxed. The War Cabinet in London received monthly reports on his progress, largely accounts of Hess's physical and, more pertinently, mental condition. When things were going badly for the Nazi war machine at the end of 1943, and an Allied victory seemed certain, the question of what to do with Hess on cessation of hostilities came up in the War Cabinet. Though Winston Churchill's attitude towards Hess had mellowed over the years he was still of the opinion the Deputy Führer should stand trial for crimes he perpetrated in the 1930s. Such a course was also demanded by Britain's European Allies, France and Soviet Russia. Joseph Stalin insisted all Nazi war criminals, and S.S. officers, should be summarily executed. Clement Attlee's Labour group in Parliament had a divergent opinion and felt Hess had served his time in captivity and should be released to return to Germany a free man. At a Tripartite Conference in Tehran in December 1943 between Roosevelt, Churchill and Stalin it became evident there would be a War Crimes Trial at cessation of hostilities and Rudolf Hess was definitely one of the top Nazi destined to be indicted. In the light of the political atmosphere at the Cabinet War Rooms, and in order to placate Attlee's supporters, the Prime Minister ordered MI6 to contrive clandestine plans for Hess's replacement with a look-alike impostor at Maindiff Court but, in his own mind, Churchill had decided to send Hess to 'face the music' at a War Crimes Tribunal.

A radical change occurred in the political set-up in Britain after July 1945's general election. Attlee's Labour Party swept into power with a thumping majority. One of Prime Minister Attlee's first actions in office in July was to give MI6 the green light to go ahead with their plans to replace Rudolf Hess with an impersonator, in German, a 'doppelgänger,' In German As a result of Attlee's late-hour intervention Rudolf Hess assumed the name, and identity, of one Ernst Prost and, as a fictional theory, he was whisked away to South America. At the same time Prost was sent to stand trial on Hess's behalf at the Palace of Justice in Nuremberg.

The mysteries concerning Rudolf Hess's flight to Britain and his subsequent behaviour in British captivity are complex and subject to conjecture not totally based on established facts. Important records of the time have still to be released by the War Office and by MI6 archivists. Taking into account the author's personal experience of regular contact with Prisoner No.7 in Spandau in 1952 and 1953, and perusing books and articles on the subject, he openly admits his suggested answers are a compilation of logical judgment on the happenings that occurred to Hess on his peace mission flight, on his captivity in Britain between May 1941 and October 1945 and his probable execution by fanatical Nazis in South America in January 1946. The identity of the convict at Nuremberg and Prisoner No.7 in Spandau, purporting to be Rudolph Hess, is a matter for further speculation and debate as is the reason for Prisoner No.7's suicide in a garden shed at the prison on 17 August 1987.

All these events are destined to remain a mystery until official records are finally released by the War Office, possibly in the year 2017. Meanwhile the enigmas concerning Hess remain controversial.

ADOLF HITLER'S AWARENESS OF HESS'S FLIGHT

The answer to this enigma is 'Yes' and 'No'!. 'Yes,' the Führer knew about Hess's intention of flying to Sweden with his peace proposals on the 10th of May, and 'No,' he did not know his Deputy was aiming for Britain. Acting in conjunction with Rudolf Hess after the fall of France in June 1940, Albrecht Haushofer made contacts with members of the Pro-peace Anglo-German League in Britain, and Heinrich Himmler, acting independently, sent Gestapo agents to consult with U.S. embassy officials in Switzerland. Rudolf Hess offered to fly to Britain with the peace proposals and the Führer reacted testily by banning him from flying for one year. Clandestine negotiation meetings in Stockholm, Madrid and Lisbon proved futile and Hitler committed himself to invading the British Isles. The Battle of Britain, and the subsequent London Blitz, put paid to any hope of a peaceful settlement between the two warring nations and, in October 1940, Hitler postponed his plans for a British invasion and concentrated his attention on an all-out assault on Soviet Russia. Slighted by the Führer's rebuff in 1940 Rudolf Hess secretly hankered after a reconciliation with the British Government. In January 1941 Adolph Hitler gave him permission to continue exploring the possibility of a peace mission flight, not to England but to a neutral destination, with Sweden as the country of choice. The Haushofer's fixed a meeting with a 'high-ranking' British diplomat in Stockholm and Hess himself wrote a letter to the Duke of Hamilton, transmitted through an intermediary source in Portugal, requesting a meeting either on 'neutral ground' or at the Duke's estate in Scotland. The letter was intercepted by MI6 and, with the Duke's cooperation, Churchill urged the British Secret

Service to play along with the request to see what might transpire. Hess's letter, however, did not reveal the identity of the proposed Nazi envoy.

Despite the Führer's flying ban Hess had made around twenty practice flights from Augsburg in a fighter loaned to him by Willi Messerschmitt, the German aircraft manufacturer. Meanwhile he had acquired two sets of accurate flight paths, one set to Stockholm and the other to the Duke of Hamilton's estate, south of Glasgow. Hess's practice flights were undertaken to familiarize himself with handling the aero plane and with his flight path from Augsburg to the German-Netherlands border. Adolf Hitler must have known about Hess's practice flights up to the North Sea. At that time he was so preoccupied with his plans to invade Russia that he failed to put a stop on Hess and the practice flights continued through March and April 1941.

On 4th May Rudolf Hess had a two-hour secret meeting with Adolf Hitler in the Chancellery in Berlin and, doubtless, their main topic for discussion revolved around Hess's proposed flight to Stockholm and the terms of the peace proposals the Nazis were prepared to offer a British delegation. Six days later, on 10th May, Hess took off from Augsburg in a Messerschmitt 110 fitted with extra fuel tanks and a radio direction compass. He had never in the past questioned, or disobeyed, the Führer's orders but, for once in his lifetime, he did so and made tracks for England on the grounds that direct access, through members of the Pro-German League and the Duke of Hamilton to possibly King George VI and the British Government, carried more clout than negotiation with a British diplomatic envoy in the Swedish capital. The Messerschmitt's 380-mile flight path over Germany and Nazi-held territory was directly north to reach the North Sea. Hess's plane then took a forty-minute diversionary course eastwards towards Sweden before he banked and flew north-westwards again across the North Sea towards the English-Scottish border. The Deputy Führer regarded himself as a knight in shining armour, flying in the face of the enemy, carrying Hitler's peace proposals and mindful, should he succeed, he would startle the World and restore himself to the forefront in the Nazi hierarchy.

Adolf Hitler received news of Hess's flight at his Berghof in Berchtesgaden on the following morning and, according to his manservant, *Herr* Henrich Linge, the Führer was fully dressed at 11:00am and evidently expecting some important information. Hitler appeared eager to get to his study and the news he was expecting was delivered in the form of a letter, hand-written by Rudolf Hess and delivered by his senior adjutant, *Oberleutenant* Karlheinz Pintsch. Expecting confirmation that Hess had flown to Stockholm Hitler went berserk when he read his Deputy had made his way to England. Albert Speer was in the Berghof at the time and recorded that the Führer ranted and raved and kept shouting and repeating, *'Mein Gott! Mein Gott!* He's deserted to England'. In Adolf Hitler's book Hess's defection amounted to desertion and, in his rage, he ordered the immediate arrest of *Oberleutenant* Karlheinz Pintsch and Albrecht Haushofer and, a week later, he decreed that, should Hess set foot in Nazi-occupied Europe, he was to be shot on sight. Pintsch was gaoled for 18 months and, on release, posted to the Russian Front. He survived the war. Professor Karl Haushofer's influence with Hitler secured Albrecht's release after a fortnight in gaol. He was re-arrested in December 1944 for his involvement in the plot to assassinate Hitler in July and he was executed by S.S. Commandos on 23rd April 1945. At the time of his death Albrecht was 42 years of age.

THE NAZI HIERARCHY AND THE FLIGHT

When the Führer realised Hess had flown to England against his explicit instructions he ordered Martin Bormann to summon the inner core of Nazi leaders to convene at the Berghof. As Hitler's private secretary, Bormann would have been aware of Hess's intention to go to Stockholm. Joachim von Ribbentrop, Germany's Foreign Minister, and Joseph Goebbels, the Propaganda Minister, were not privy to the exact details of the mission but became crucial in advising the Führer on the subsequent cover-up story. Heinrich Himmler, Head of the Gestapo, had his own agenda for contacting the Allies to discuss peace terms and his ideas included spiriting Hitler away into exile with himself taking over as Führer of Germany. Hitler would have kept the Gestapo chief informed about Hess's intended peace mission to Sweden. The Nazi bigwig who knew all the details about Hess's mission was *Reichsairmarschal* Hermann Göering. As early as July 1940, when Rudolf Hess first proposed flying to England to seek an armistice, Göering offered the services of his Luftwaffe to blast the Deputy Führer's plane out of the sky. No love was lost between Göering and Hess and, in May 1941, the *Reichsairmarschal* again offered his services pointing out that his 'ace' fighter pilot, Major Adolf Galland, was conveniently based at Germany's northern coast and in position to intercept Hess's plane. Hitler again refused Göering's offer and pointed out that such an action would not be necessary, as his Deputy Führer had only been given permission to fly to neutral Sweden. Significantly, on the day of Hess's flight, all German radio communications with the Baltic States were blocked for ten hours.

On 10th May 1941 Rudolf Hess's chief adjutant, Karlheinz Pintsch, waited a statutory four hours at the Messerschmitt airstrip in Augsburg and, when it was evident Hess's plane was not returning, he rang the Air Ministry in Berlin to inquire about weather conditions in Scotland. His phone call rang alarm bells and *Reichsairmarschal* Göering was informed. Without consulting Hitler, Göering ordered Adolf Galland's fighter wing to take to the air and shoot down Hess's Messerschmitt. It was nearly 10pm when Göering issued the frantic order and darkness was beginning to descend over Northern Germany. Galland's fighters failed in their hopeless mission and Hess's Messerschmitt was well out of their range. In his book on his wartime experiences titled 'The First and the Last', published in 1953, Galland made light of Göering's derisory order. He realised from the start that an attempt at an interception would be futile and, as a token gesture, ordered only four fighter planes into the air to search for the Deputy Führer's Messerschmitt. Galland was forced to inform Göering that his planes had failed on their hapless mission.

BRITISH INTELLIGENCE'S AWARENESS OF THE FLGHT

Soon after the Dunkirk evacuation, and the fall of France in June 1940, a Pro-peace faction in the British Government, and aristocratic members of an Anglo-German League, began agitating for a quick, and peaceful, settlement to the conflict with Nazi Germany. Prime Minister Winston Churchill was fully aware of these agitators and his rabble-rousing wartime speeches were directed towards the pacifists as well as bolstering morale in British citizens. Prominent among the peace movement were a few members of the British aristocracy -- Lord Halifax and the Duke of Bedford in the House of Lords and Rab Butler and Sir Samuel Hoare in the House of Commons. Foreign Office and MI6 agents in the embassies of neutral countries in Europe acted as facilitators, arranging clandestine meetings between British diplomats and their Nazi counterparts. The feverish secret activity during the summer of 1940 gradually abated only to be rekindled in December 1940 by a letter from Hess to the Duke of Hamilton, a wartime Squadron Leader in the Royal Air Force and stationed outside Edinburgh, requesting a meeting with a high-ranking British delegate to discuss a peace treaty between the two nations. The letter was intercepted by MI6 and landed up on the Prime Minister's table. Churchill agreed it was probably another Nazi hoax and made a decision "to go along with it and to see what transpires".

The maverick plane carrying the mysterious envoy came within local radar range of Northumbria at around 10:20pm and fighter squadrons in the north of England, and in Scotland, were alerted to shadow the Messerschmitt but to allow its free passage; a Czech squadron from Northern Ireland took off and was hastily ordered to return to base; landing lights at Dungavel airstrip were allegedly meant to be displayed by secret agents, or members of the Pro-peace group, to assist the plane's descent but this did not happen. A few members of the disbanded 1930s Anglo-German League congregated in the locality of Dungavel, presumably to receive the Nazi envoy. Surprisingly the Duke of Kent and the Duke of Buccleach were involved in a minor road accident just outside the gates to Dungavel on 10th May 1941. All these pointers indicate that MI6 agents, and ex-members of the Anglo-German League, were expecting an important visitor from Germany on that night.

On Sunday morning, 11th May 1941, it was established that Hitler's peace envoy was none other than Germany's Deputy

Führer, Rudolf Hess. A transatlantic telephone link between the Cabinet War Rooms and the White House in Washington was buzzing for days after Hess's arrival in Britain and the British PM and President Roosevelt agreed on his management in captivity. It soon became clear to MI6 interrogators that the Deputy Führer was unable, or deliberately declined, to provide any useful information about Hitler's plans for the future conduct of the war, The American President lost all interest in the Nazi defector and delegated his further management to the British Government. At a conference at Yalta in February 1945, Roosevelt became aware that Hess was included on a list of top Nazis to stand trial after the war. The President sadly died in office six weeks later and was succeeded by Harry S. Truman and, in July 1945, Clement Attlee succeeded Winston Churchill as Prime Minister after a landslide election victory by the Labour Party. There is no tangible evidence that the two 'new' Western leaders enjoyed the same relationship as Roosevelt and Churchill. Whether President Truman, and the U.S. Secret Service, had prior knowledge of the 'switch' at Maindiff Court on 9th October 1945 is a closely guarded secret and it is highly probable the British Government might have acted on its own initiative. When President Truman met with Stalin and Prime Minister Attlee at a Potsdam Conference in July 1945, and the fate of the Nazi leaders was discussed and finalised, he had more pressing worries on his mind. He was preoccupied with bringing the Pacific War to a conclusion by taking responsibility for ordering the Atomic Bomb attack on the Japanese mainland.

BRITAIN'S WARTIME COALITION CABINET AND RUDOLF HESS

A charismatic wartime Prime Minister, and brilliant orator, Sir Winston Churchill had his failings and, despite his undoubted courage in saving Britain from German occupation in 1940, some of his decisions were risky and hastily constructed. He was kind at heart but took umbrage readily and this trait was clearly demonstrated in his dealings with Rudolf Hess. When the Nazi pilot who landed in Scotland on May 10th 1941 was positively identified as Rudolf Hess, Winston Churchill was jubilant. He behaved like a schoolboy who had landed his first big trout and was determined to bleed the Deputy Führer dry of information. But Rudolf Hess did not cooperate. Despite Clement Attlee's protestations it was Churchill's decision to transfer Hess to the Tower of London and to appoint MI6's chief interrogator, Major Frank Foley, to question him. In the Tower Hess was treated like a spy and was made forcibly aware that *Herren* Meier and Waldberg, Nazi espionage agents, had been executed at the Tower as recently as December 1940. Rudolf Hess shut up like a clam. Attlee was furious and persuaded the Prime Minister to change tactics. Hess was reclassified as an officer prisoner-of-war and, to placate Attlee, Churchill ordered he was to be detained under close arrest and guarded by His Majesty's Footguards. He was given all privileges accorded to a senior ranking officer in the German army but interrogation by Major Frank Foley's MI6 team was to continue. Clement Attlee agreed to these arrangements.

Winston Churchill had a further change of heart when Hess attempted suicide at Mytchett Place on 15th June 1941 and suffered a fractured femur. There were now serious concerns about the Deputy Führer's mental stability. The Cabinet agreed he should be treated as a medical patient but the Prime Minister insisted his interrogation should continue unabated. Hess's mental condition deteriorated and a decision was made in January 1942 to transfer him from Mytchett Place to a military, mental-cum-convalescent hospital at Abergavenny in South Wales. By now Churchill had given Hess up as a lost cause. Clement Attlee was advocating repatriation of the sick Nazi but Churchill refused on the grounds that Adolf Hitler had declared that, if Hess set foot in Nazi-occupied Europe, he was to be shot on sight. For three and a half years at Maindiff Court Hospital the main contact between the patient and the British War Cabinet was a monthly report on Hess's general and mental health.

Winston Churchill returned in a foul mood after meeting with Stalin in Moscow on November 6th 1944. "Uncle Joe" had insinuated he was lying when he refuted any knowledge beforehand of the Deputy Führer's flight to Britain and that an invitation to Hess to come to England existed before he left Germany. Stalin believed Hess had played a vital part in organizing Operation Barabarossa – the German invasion of Soviet Russia in June 1941. It now seemed certain Rudolf Hess would stand trial after the war and, if the Russians had their way, he would be executed. At Cabinet meetings Attlee pleaded for clemency to the ailing Deputy Führer. In a pique Churchill agreed they should set the wheels in motion to make plans to protect Hess from the wrath of Stalin and the Soviet Politburo. MI6 were entrusted with the task of investigating all means to achieve their goal and came up with a plan to replace Hess at Maindiff Hospital with an impostor. Anxious to repay "Uncle Joe" for his unjust accusations Churchill felt relieved something had been done to put Stalin's nose out of joint. He still insisted, however, that should the subterfuge fail Hess would have to stand trial with the rest of the top Nazis.

A year later, the three leaders met at Yalta in January 1945. President Roosevelt was a sick man and gave way too easily to

Stalin's territorial demands. The Soviet Union annexed the whole of Eastern Europe and Berlin was included within the Russian zone of influence. Churchill was appalled by the outcome of the meeting but he was forced to give way. Rudolf Hess was entry No.2 on a list of around forty senior Nazi war criminals drawn up by the Three Power delegates. It was agreed the War Crimes Tribunal would be held at Nuremberg at the cessation of hostilities. Furious with the outcome of the Yalta Conference, Churchill now saw the cunning fox in the Kremlin in a different light and later described the situation as "An 'Iron Curtain' descending across Europe." Churchill met Attlee in secret and, with his sense of guile and intrigue, suggested plans to replace Hess with an impostor should be activated. He stressed, however, that this could not be done immediately as, for official consumption, he had given his word to Joseph Stalin that the Deputy Führer would appear for trial at Nuremberg. Whether the American President was privy to the deception is not clear. Roosevelt was a dying man and passed away in April 1945. His successor was Harry. S. Truman and, three months later, Churchill's Tory Party lost a general election. Clement Attlee's first action as Prime Minister in July 1945 was to authorise MI6 to go ahead urgently to replace Rudolf Hess at Maindiff Court Hospital with an impostor. In the doldrums and depth of despair after losing the General Election Winston Churchill was in full agreement with the new Prime Minister's action, which exonerated the wartime Prime Minister from his promise to Joseph Stalin.

IDENTTY OF THE NAZI PILOT WHO LANDED IN SCOTLAND.

Dr Hugh Thomas has made a fascinating case for suggesting the man who parachuted to the ground at Eaglesham in

Scotland at around 11.10 pm on 10th May 1941 was an impostor and not Germany's Deputy Führer. There is no controversy about the identity of the man who took off from Augsburg in a Messerschmitt 110. Rudolf Hess was a competent aviator and, more importantly, a meticulous and accurate navigator. Presuming the envoy who floated to earth in Scotland was an impostor, Hess's plane would have to be dispatched over the North Sea and the impostor's aircraft would have to complete its flight from Denmark to Scotland, a complicated, far-fetched and involved theory. Discovering a Hess look-alike would not have been impossible, as the Deputy Führer had employed three, or four, during his time in office in the 1930's. However, to find a suitable impostor, who could fly a Messerschmitt fighter and navigate it to within 15 miles of its intended destination, would be a miracle and well-nigh impossible. Added to all these improbabilities the time limit, about a fortnight, to brief the impostor about Hess's life history, achievements, social and political contacts and personal peccadilloes, would have been a mammoth task. The person who came to earth at Floors Farm near Eaglesham in Renfrewshire, and spent the rest of the war in captivity in Britain, was definitely Rudolf Hess. A further pointer to his identity was the prisoner's repeated requests at Maindiff Court Hospital to visit his aunt's grave at Michaelstone-y-Fedw, outside Cardiff. His 'aunt' died and was buried in 1891 three years before Hess was born and it is extremely doubtful that an impostor would have been told this fact before he embarked on a flight to intercept Hess's Messerchmitt and proceed onwards to Scotland and captivity.

Identity Of The Nazi Prisoner In Nuremberg And Spandau

The author has advanced a plausible theory that the man who was taken for trial at Nuremberg was not Rudolf Hess and that a 'switch' occurred at Maindiff Court Hospital on the night of the 9th May 1941. Assuming his theory is correct, the fate of the "real" Hess needs explanation. The author's fictitious contention is that Hess took on the identity and full name of one of his look-alikes from the 1930s and, with British connivance and almost certainly American knowledge, he was whisked away to South America in October 1945 and met his death at the hands of fanatic exiled Nazi SS zealots in January 1946. The author's suggestion for Hess's eventual fate may be not too far off the mark considering the known aggressiveness and antipathy towards deserters, and in their view traitors, exhibited by these ex-SS henchmen.

The Mental Problems Of Prisoner No.7 In Spandau

Part of the author's Regimental duties with the Welsh Guards in Berlin was to provide medical cover for Spandau Prison and he had the opportunity to see 'Hess', and six other Nazi war criminals, on a daily basis in each of three separate months in 1952 and 1953. Around forty visits to the prison were conducted like a military sick parade and bore little resemblance to a traditional hospital ward round. Accompanied by a warder the inmates were approached and stood to attention wherever they were sitting, reading, gardening or walking and he was only allowed to ask one question – "Any complaints, No. X?" Most times the inmates never replied and further action on the author's part was only required on rare occasions. He only examined Prisoner No 7 once – it was one freezing night in January 1953. He was called to Spandau in the early hours to see "Hess" as an emergency. "Hess" was in his cell, writhing on his bed shouting loudly and complaining of abdominal pain. The author examined the prisoner's abdomen in poor lighting in the ice-cold cell. He has been asked on several occasions if he found any evidence of bullet wound scars on the left side of his chest at his examination. The answer is simple. The icy conditions and poor lighting in No 7's cell that night were not conducive to a full-body examination.

The author's experience in providing medical cover for Spandau's Nazi war criminals is sometimes a subject for discussion and a question invariably asked is "Was Prisoner No 7 mad?" Madness is defined as insanity in a subject prone to derangement of the mind and demonstrating violent sensations, emotions or ideas. As a recently qualified doctor with a main interest in a surgical career, the author's experience in psychiatry during his medical training had been minimal. His layman's diagnosis of Prisoner No 7's mental condition in 1952 was that he was "bonkers," not mad, not insane, but had a queer, eccentric personality and an odd human being. He was unapproachable and never smiled during the time he knew him. It was not rocket science to diagnose that Prisoner No 7 was suffering from paranoia and depression and these diagnoses had been the opinions of at least a dozen eminent psychiatrists who had examined Rudolf Hess at Mytchett Place, and Maindiff Court and during the Nuremberg trial. The author had no reason in 1952 to cast any doubts on the fact that Prisoner No 7 was not Rudolf Hess. However, he has since become converted to the belief that the inmate in cell No 7 at Spandau was an impostor. He can only conclude that it speaks volumes for Prisoner No 7's determination, single-mindedness and acting ability, to convince everyone around him for all those years in captivity that he was, in fact, Walter Rudolf Richard Hess.

THE IMPOSTOR'S 41-YEAR DECEPTION

The impostor selected by MI6 to replace Hess had been picked up in Hamburg's Red Light District in July 1945. Ernst Prost had been one of Rudolf Hess's main stand-ins in the 1930s and earned his living in Vaudeville theatres impersonating the Deputy Führer. He had worked closely with Hess until Rudolf's defection to Britain on 10th May 1941. Afterwards the impersonator became a persona non grata with the Nazi Party. In 1944 an attempted revival of Hess's vaudeville sketch led to a six-month jail sentence and, after Prost's release from prison, he lived in constant fear of persecution, and probable extermination, by the Gestapo. By January 1945 Prost had escaped from Berlin to Hamburg and another, equally dangerous, threat loomed on the horizon. Soviet Russia believed Rudolf Hess had been a major player in planning Operation Barbarossa, the German attack on the USSR in June 1941. Hess was one of their major targets for execution after the war ended and, due to his spitting-image likeness to the Deputy Führer, Prost had little doubt about his fate if the advancing Russian armies captured him. He welcomed approaches from an MI6 agent in Hamburg in July and willingly accompanied him to England and semi-captivity. The impostor had concluded he would be in safer hands in Britain than taking the risk of remaining in Germany. Rudolf Hess had been Ernst Prost's idol in his heyday in Nazi Germany in the 1930's and, when he met his hero face-to-face at Maindiff Court in September 1945, he readily agreed to impersonate his mentor once again even if it meant facing a War Crimes Tribunal on his behalf.

Appearing in the dock at Nuremberg the impostor exceeded all expectations in his acting ability and, employing memory loss as a trusty shield, he fooled the judiciary, the guards, prison authorities, medical experts and, more pertinently, most of Hess's former brethren in the Nazi party. Prost was given carte blanche by MI6, and the British Government, to reveal his true identity at any time, but when he escaped the gallows and was awarded a life sentence at the Tribunal, so imbued was he by his successful impersonation of Rudolf Hess he made up his mind to continue with the charade for a few more months. As it transpired the months were extended to years.

An incredible situation arose on his arrival at Spandau Prison in August 1947 where he continued fooling the authorities, the guards, the warders and his fellow inmates. As a down-at-heel actor, with no prospects outside prison, he gloried in being a member of the elite cadre of criminals incarcerated at Spandau and thoughts of reveling his identity were put on the back burner. For 19 years at Spandau the impostor had companions but after December 1966, when Albert Speer and Baldur von Schirach were released, he became the sole occupant at the prison for the next 21 years. As the years rolled by the impostor became institutionalized. He suffered from prison psychosis, a dependency on a rigid prison regime, and he developed a morbid fear of being released into the outside world to face intimate contacts with Hess's family and friends. One conclusion from this evidence is that Prisoner No 7 felt safe and secure at Spandau Prison and developed a fear of facing the outside world. He voluntarily remained a prison inmate in Spandau for 41 years, a tragic figure, guarded by Regiments from the Four Powers. This costly exercise was perpetrated year after year largely to satisfy the East German and Russian demands for a legitimate foothold in West Berlin.

For the forty-one years the impostor was incarcerated at Spandau Prison the British Government and MI6 were content to let sleeping dogs lie. In their estimation revealing Prisoner No 7's true identity would severely compromise improving relations between Britain and the U.S.S.R. The terminal crisis came on 17th August 1987 when the 92-year-old prisoner ended his life in a garden hut at the prison. The British authorities quickly arranged for an Army Special Branch team to investigate the suspected suicide and a British Home Office pathologist to conduct the autopsy. A strong case has been advanced by the author to conclude that Prisoner No7 was too frail and arthritic to hang himself and that he was assisted in the final act by a "friendly" warder. Rudolf Hess's impersonator probably met his death by assisted euthanasia, a joint venture almost certainly orchestrated by British and American secret agents.

British authorities failed to get permission from the War Crimes Commission to cremate the body, which would have finally destroyed all evidence of Prisoner No. 7's identity. His remains, however, were exhumed twice after his first internment and DNA sampling was refused on both occasions. The final act in this fascinating saga is yet to come. The answers to the enigmas in Rudolf Hess's life are protected in secret Foreign Office and MI6 files, possibly not due for release to the public until the year 2017. These files may establish that Prisoner No 7 in Nuremberg and Spandau was an impostor and the enigmas about what happened to Germany's Deputy Führer may remain unsolved forever. The author's fictitious description, outlining Hess's fate at the hands of fanatic S.S. Nazis exiles in Uruguay and Argentina in January 1946 may well be as accurate an account as any and not too far removed from the truth.

ADDENDUM – JULY 2012

Conspiracy theorists were given a fillip when, as a result of pressure to release secret MI6 files and applications to the Freedom of Information Act, two reports appeared simultaneously in the March 17th 2012 issues of the Daily Telegraph and The Times, providing proof that a mass of secret information still exists about Rudolf Hess and Prisoner No.7 at Spandau. Both articles dealt substantially with the controversy surrounding Prisoner No 7's alleged suicide at Spandau with only passing reference to the other contentious arguing point, No 7's true identity. Most of the information contained declassified reports compiled by the Special Investigation Branch of the British Military Police and their conclusions as to the cause of death. The investigating SIB team arrived at Spandau within 24 hours of Prisoner No.7's suspected suicide and their report was available at a post-mortem examination conducted at the British Military Hospital on the following day. Wolf Rüdiger, Rudolf Hess's 49-year-old son, insisted from the beginning his 'father' was murdered by MI6 and American agents in order to prevent his release and disclosure of the truth behind his defection and mercy mission to Britain in May 1941. He conducted his own investigation into his 'father's' suspected suicide and encountered Russian obstruction all along the line.

By August 1987 Prisoner No 7 at Spandau was a frail, arthritic nonagenarian. His frailty made it impossible for him to commit suicide unaided. Arguably Prisoner No 7 was an impostor. It is the author's contention that British and American Governments were fully aware of this fact and, together, plotted to prevent No. 7 disclosing his identity to the Soviet authorities and the World. As General Secretary of the Russian Politburo, Mikael Gorbachev was considering "Hess's" release in 1986 and, having successfully protected his true identity for 42 years, British and American secret agencies combined to formulate a plan of assisted euthanasia. For all intents and purposes Prisoner No. 7's suicide was meant to look self-inflicted, an impossible act considering the frail state of the victim and his lack of manual dexterity.

There are several discrepancies in the Special Investigation Branch's inquiry into Prisoner No. 7's death. The yellow cable used in the suicide had been left in the garden summerhouse by electricity workmen and was not an extension to a reading lamp used by No.7, as claimed by the SIB. The warder who accompanied No.7 into the garden hut on his final walk was simply labeled "2" in the SIB report. Anthony Jordan was the warder in question and the SIB recorded that "2" was absent from the hut for only 5 minutes, whereas Jordan left No. 7 unattended for at least 15 minutes, allegedly to make, or receive, a phone call in the main office block. When he returned to the hut Jordan found No. 7 half-crouched on the floor with the electric flex tight around his neck. He was blue in the face and, though the "drop" was just over 4ft, compression on his neck, his death struggle and his frail condition had led to his eventual strangulation. The Military Police investigation concluded – "There were no marks, or material of evidential value, to suggest criminal involvement of any person." A quandary remains as to why the SIB reports referred to "2" and not to Anthony Jordan by name. It begs the question if the SIB were acting under orders from higher authority to protect Jordan's name appearing in transcripts of No. 7's suicide. The SIB also appears to have fallen short on one major issue – they failed to, or were under orders to desist from, interrogating witnesses and, in particular, Anthony Jordan. If they had done so one has to assume that part of their documents are secret and still held in the MOD or MI6 archives. Up until the newspaper articles of 17th July 2012, it was assumed no photographs, or fingerprints, of No.7's cadaver and the suicide location, existed. It was understood the SIB had been denied permission to undertake these examinations, both routine investigations in any suicide case. Writing in the Daily Mail of Friday 27th July, Dr Hugh T Thomas reported that photographs were taken by an unknown authority, which showed the instrument of strangulation, the electric flex, lying in close proximity to No.7's body. The SIB concluded incorrectly the strangulating instrument had been a coil of flex connected to a reading lamp. Information from fingerprinting was apparently denied to the SIB and whether secret information from this source is still being held in Whitehall remains to be seen. According to Dr Thomas the cadaver photographs did not show any evidence of scarring as a result of gunshot wounds to the left chest, suffered by Rudolf Hess at Focsani, in Romania, in August, and recorded by a hospital medical officer in December. By order of the Prison Commandant the garden shed was razed to the ground 48 hours following the suicide and all its contents, including the incriminating electric flex, were destroyed.

Prisoner No.7's suicide note was declared authentic by a handwriting expert. It had to be accepted that the prisoner's handwriting had deteriorated over the years, undoubtedly aggravated by arthritis of the finger joints and a weakened grip in his left hand. No. 7's farewell letter to his family was hardly the death wish of a devoted husband. He merely thanked all his dear ones for all they had done for him. Prisoner No.7's letter was more concerned about his behavior towards one of Hess's favorite female secretaries at the Braunhaus in Munich in the 1930's. "Freiburg" was Rudolf's pet name for Hildegard Fath and, when she visited No.7 in Nuremberg before the Trial began, he alleged 'the Nuremberg process had forced him to act as if he did not know her.' He ended the suicide letter by thanking 'Freiburg', and his family, for the pictures they had sent him and signed the letter *Euer Grosher*," "Your Eldest". If Prisoner No.7 was an impostor he would clearly remember Hildegard Fath's visit to his cell at the Palace of Justice. He deliberately pleaded amnesia to avoid trying to recall intimate memories of Rudolf Hess's family life at Munich. This remains one of the many pointers that Prisoner No. 7 at Spandau was not Rudolf Hess.

Another pointer to the Special Investigation Branch's assumed superficiality in examining Prisoner No 7's body and clothing has recently been highlighted by the Freedom of Information Act. On the day he committed suicide Prisoner No 7 was dressed in a grey suit, white shirt and long-johns, blue socks and brown shoes. On his head he wore a sombrero and carried a walking stick in his right hand. All his clothing and appendages were handed to the Prison Governor for disposal immediately after the post-mortem. Only No. 7's dentures were retained by the B.M.H Dental Department. The clothing and appendages might have given valuable clues as to the identity of the prisoner in Cell No.7 at Spandau. It would have been standard practice for SIB investigators to strip the body for a thorough examination of the clothing but it is likely they were refused permission to do so. At the autopsy at the B.M.H. the body was presented fully clothed with an endotracheal tube still in situ. To everyone's surprise a suicide note was found in the tunic's right hand pocket. This poses the question, 'Was the suicide note present in No. 7's coat pocket at the S.I.B's preliminary inspection at the B.M.H or did they fail to inspect the jacket?'

Another mysterious order by the prison authorities demanded a complete ban on photography of the scene of the tragedy and of the cadaver at post-mortem examination. Recent evidence confirms that photographs were taken at the crime scene at Spandau and it would not be beyond belief to assume that the cadaver was also photographed in detail. The SIB's hands were probably tied and they may have been denied permission to carry out routine procedures practiced in the investigation of a suspected criminal death. On the other hand if photographs of Prisoner No. 7's cadaver do exist they have not as yet been released by Whitehall. They may show incriminating evidence to establish the identity of the dead Nazi impersonator.

Prisoner No. 7 was first buried by the family a week after his autopsies at a secret grave in the Fitchel Mountains. On 17th March 1988 he was exhumed and re-interred in the family plot at Wunsiedel. In the late1990's extreme right-wing neo-Nazis came to champion 'Hess' as a martyr and believed he was murdered at Spandau and that his mission to Britain in 1941 was a heroic gesture deserving the highest respect of the Nazi dynasty. The family plot at Wunsiedel became a place of worship for the pseudo-Nazi zealots. Their annual pilgrimages developed into riots and the local council obtained permission to exhume the remaining body parts in August 2011. After cremation, No.7's ashes were scattered over the North Sea. For the purpose of D.N.A. assessment Prisoner No. 7's remains had become available after two exhumations between 1992 and 2011. His body parts were the property of the Hess family and, on each occasion, they strongly objected to subjecting their charge to any genetic tests. The British and American Governments were perfectly satisfied to concur with the Hess family's wishes to deny DNA examination on the cadaver.

Release of classified information in July 2012 has cast some light on the actions of the authorities at the time of Prisoner No. 7's suicide. Many conspiracy theorists maintain that No. 7 was murdered in the garden shed at Spandau Prison on the 17th August 1987. Acceptance of their theories is tantamount to believing the Special Investigation Branch of the Royal Military Police were ordered by higher authority only to conduct a superficial investigation into No. 7's suicide. The secret has been propagated for 25 years by the British MI6 and the American CIA on behalf of their respective Governments. There may be secret revelations to come and whether these will cast light on the identity of Prisoner No. 7, and whether he was murdered or dispatched by assisted euthanasia, are fascinating unsolved mysteries that have challenged the conspiracy theorists for over six decades.

EPILOGUE

The author's intention in publishing this book is to acquaint readers with Rudolf Hess's life story. Beginning with his birth in Alexandria in Egypt, and his schooling in private academies in Germany and Switzerland, then on to his service in the German Army and his serious gunshot wound during World War I. Afterwards came his enrolment at Munich University, and in the fledgling Nazi Party in 1920; his eventual rise to power within the Party, in the shadow of Adolf Hitler, to become Germany's Deputy Führer in 1934. His story continued with his flight to Scotland on the 10th of May 1941 – ostensibly on a secret mission to present Adolf Hilter's peace terms to the British Government - and his incarceration for 14 months at Mytchett Place, Aldershot and for a further 39 months at Maindiff Court Hospital near Abergavenny. One author questioned the identity of the German pilot held in custody in Britain between May 1941 and the 10th of October 1945. An overwhelming majority of authorities are firmly of the opinion that the Nazi airman who flew from Augsburg in Germany to Scotland was truly the 'real' Walter Rudolf Richard Hess.

From May 1952 to June 1953 the author was a Medical Officer to Spandau Prison which involved around forty-five prison visits when his Welsh Guards Battalion was on guard duty. At the time he did not entertain any thoughts to disbelieve that the convict in cell No. 7 was not Rudolf Hess. In recent years the author's mind was changed and he now firmly believes the "Hess" he looked after medically in 1952-53 was an impostor. He has become convinced that successive American and British Governments, and their Secret Services, have conspired to conceal the fact that convict 125 at the Nuremberg trial, and Prisoner No.7 in Spandau, was an impostor. The author's fictional theory describes Rudolf Hess's transportation from Maindiff Court on the 9th October 1945 after a 'switch' occurred at the hospital. The ex-Deputy Führer was conceivably spirited away to South America and an impostor took his place and was dispatched to the Palace of Justice in Nuremberg on the 10th October to stand trial on Hess's behalf.

The author's current belief rests on reliable medical evidence of the absence of scars on No.7's left chest, the impostor's behavior in captivity in Nuremberg and Spandau and the conspiracy still existing about Prisoner No. 7's alleged suicide in prison on the 17th August 1987. On the day of his admission to the Palace of Justice, "Hess" was given a thorough examination by U.S. resident medical officer, Major Ben Horewitz. Two autopsies were conducted on Prisoner No.7 after his alleged suicide, one by a senior British Army Pathologist and the second, at the Hess family's request, by a German Professor of Pathology. A critical observation was made at the British Military Hospital's x-ray department in September 1973 when Prisoner No.7 attended for radiology examinations. Major H. T. Thomas looked specifically for scars on the patient's left chest and found none, supporting Major Horewitz's negative clinical findings in 1946 and the two autopsies performed by senior Pathologists in 1987. These negative medical pointers form the basis for the author's conviction that No. 7 at Spandau was not Rudolf Hess.

Released under the Freedom of Information Act, and

published in the Daily Telegraph of 7th April 2012, Dr Henry V Dicks's private notes, abstracted from psychiatric archives, reveal the extent of Rudolf Hess's Jewish antipathy. Dr Dicks was Hess's personal psychiatrist at Mytchett Place from May 1941 to July 1942. 'Jonathan' had confided in Dicks that he was the only person with psychic powers enabling him to appreciate the power of Jewish evil forces who were attempting to kill him and were instrumental in hypnotising Britain's wartime leaders, including Winston Churchill. Hess also argued Jews would have hypnotised guards and warders to behave cruelly in the Concentration Camps, if such establishments ever existed in Germany.

Twenty-three indicted Nazi war criminals were incarcerated at the Palace of Justice for 12 months before they were sentenced on the 1st October 1946 for their nefarious activities during World War II. Seven were transferred to Spandau Prison in August 1947 and twelve condemned to death by hanging. The Nuremberg Tribunal lasted for eleven months and, during this period, it is of significance to note that Hermann Göering and Joachim von Ribbentrop repeatedly questioned the true identity of the convict in cell 125. Controversy remains as to why the prison authorities, and legal experts, took no action to investigate the claims of two of Rudolf Hess's major pre-war colleagues in the Nazi Party. At Nuremberg the impostor was forced to meet Professor Haushofer and Rudolf Hess's female private secretaries from Munich. He pleaded loss of memory at the meetings. He refused to write to Rudolf Hess's family. He refused to give a blood sample and a specimen signature. The impostor's denial to accept family visits at Spandau Prison continued for 22 years until November 1969 when he was seriously ill in the British Military Hospital. He was admitted as an emergency with a suspected perforated peptic ulcer. Near death's door, the impostor allowed a visit by Rudolf Hess's wife and son on Christmas Eve 1969. Thereafter sporadic visits occurred up until his 'suicide' in August 1987. A devoted family man, Rudolf Hess would never have treated his dearest ones so shabbily and the only logical conclusion is the impostor contrived to avoid meeting face-to-face with Hess's kith and kin. His lukewarm suicide note also bears testimony to his desire to keep the Hess family at a distance.

Another strong pointer to his identity occurred within a few weeks of his arrival at Nuremberg. Rudolf Hess became a strict vegetarian convert in the late 1920's. A varied diet was available to the Nazi convicts awaiting trial at the Palace of Justice and it soon became evident that Convict 125 regularly selected hearty, protein-laden meals. The impostor had been weaned on to a vegetarian regime during his ten weeks in Britain but the attraction of a liberal diet at Nuremberg overcame his vegetarian prejudices. He continued eating meat and fish at Spandau on the rare occasions when protein products were available on the spartan menus. This reversion to the norm is regarded as a pertinent clue to No.7's true identity.

Investigations into No. 7's alleged suicide seemed on the surface to be a botched affair. The actual 'suicide' occurred during the American duty month at Spandau which suggests the U.S. authorities had a leading role in overseeing the final act. Their agent on the ground was almost certainly one Anthony Jordan, No. 7's prison warder. When his death had been confirmed, British authorities took over and called in an investigation team and arranged the autopsy, both functions carried out with apparent haste and within 48 hours of the event. The Special Investigation Branch of the Royal British

Military Police seem to have only made a cursory examination of the suicide location and of the corpse and concluded No. 7's death was not due to any external agencies. They omitted, or were banned by the prison authorities, to interview Anthony Jordan, a key witness in their investigations. The British pathologists' autopsy report described No. 7's death as being due to self-inflicted strangulation confirmed, at the Hess family's request, by a private post-mortem conducted by a German Professor of Pathology two days later. Neither autopsy, carried out by expert forensic pathologists, recorded scars on No.7's left chest which would aid in identifying the victim as Rudolf Hess. British plans to cremate No. 7's corpse immediately after the autopsy at the B.M.H. were thwarted by Four-Power Prison Commissioners. After the Hess family's private post-mortem examination on 21st August 1987, the impostor's body was buried in a secret grave on the Fitchel Mountains in Franconia.

Hess's relatives exhumed the body and re-interred it in a family plot at Wunsiedel in March 1988. The report in the Daily Telegraph on 20th July 2011 indicated that the last opportunity to positively identify the corpse by DNA sampling had been lost forever. Due to unwelcome pilgrimages by Nazi fanatics Hess's relatives were given permission to re-exhume Prisoner No. 7's remains for a second time on 20th August 2011. After cremation his ashes were scattered over the North Sea. For the second time in 19 years the opportunity for DNA identification was missed. Rudolf Hess's family were accused of objecting to a DNA analysis by the Foreign Office whose MI6 department still harbor secret files amongst their classified archives. The contents of those files will definitely throw further light on the enigmas surrounding Rudolf Hess and the final act in this fascinating saga is yet to come. If it is finally established the body interred at Wunsiedel was that of an impostor the mystery about Rudolf Hess's disappearance may never be solved and the author's fictional account, outlining his fate at the hands of fanatic SS Nazi exiles in Uruguay and Argentina, may not be far removed from the truth.

The most compelling identity pointer to Prisoner No.7 occurred during the Nuremberg Tribunal. Joachim von Ribbentrop and Hermann Göering were dubious about convict "Hess's" identity at the Trial. When asked a question about Hess by a prosecuting barrister Hermann Göering hit the nail on its head and replied with a sly, conceited smirk "Hess? Which Hess? The Hess you have here? Our Hess? Your Hess?" In this context, "Our Hess" obviously referred to Adolf Hitler's Deputy Führer. Göering and von Ribbentrop had known and worked closely with Rudolf Hess during the Nazi Party's rise to power and Adolf Hilter's dictatorship in the 1930's. "Your Hess" insinuated that the convict, sitting in the dock between Göering and von Ribbentrop at the Nuremberg trial, was a British stool pigeon indoctrinated by their Secret Service and not the 'real' Walter Rudolf Richard Hess. Inexplicably the prison authorities and judiciary avoided inquiries to substantiate the Nazi convicts' suspicions. On the balance of accumulated evidence available for inspection at the present time, Hermann Göering's and von Ribberntrops's genuine suspicions lend the strongest support to the doppelgänger theorists and is a major pointer to the identity of Prisoner No.7 at Spandau

About The Author

A native from Carmarthenshire in West Wales, Eric Sturdy studied medicine at Guy's Hospital and qualified in April 1950. During National Service, in 1952 and 1953, he was Medical Officer to the 1st Battalion Welsh Guards, stationed in Berlin. For three separate months the Guards provided sentries for Spandau Prison. During these months the author was a Prison M.O. and was required to make frequent visits to the seven Nazi war criminals in Spandau, including 'Rudolf Hess.' On returning to civilian life he enlisted in the Territorial Army attaining the rank of lieutenant Colonel in the Royal Army Medical Corps. Eric pursued a career in surgery and practiced as a Consultant General Surgeon at the Royal Gwent Hospital, Newport for 31 years retiring in May 1993. His hobbies in retirement are fiction writing and fishing. Eric has been happily married to Meriel for 59 years. They had three children, seven grandchildren and a gorgeous three year old great grandchild.

Additional Historical Fiction By The Author

Blood Brothers
ISBN-10: 1861060963   ISBN-13: 9781861060969
pseudonym David E Scott (pub. 1997)

The Bulldog, the Whippet, the Bat and the Falcon
ISBN-10: 0754109240   ISBN-13: 9780754109242
pseudonym David E Scott (pub. 1999)

Operation Gan
ISBN-10: 0954444906   ISBN-13: 9780954444907
D Eric Sturdy (pub. 2003)

Vendetta
ISBN 9780954444914
D Eric Sturdy (pub. 2008)

Lightning Source UK Ltd.
Milton Keynes UK
UKOW04n0126041214

242593UK00003B/52/P